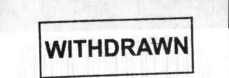

WHAT BECOMES

WHAT BECOMES

A.L. Kennedy

JONATHAN CAPE
LONDON

Published by Jonathan Cape 2009

2 4 6 8 10 9 7 5 3 1

First published in Great Britain in 2009 by
Jonathan Cape
Random House, 20 Vauxhall Bridge Road,
London SW1V 2SA

www.rbooks.co.uk

Addresses for companies within The Random House Group Limited
can be found at: www.randomhouse.co.uk/offices.htm

The Random House Group Limited Reg. No. 954009

A CIP catalogue record for this book is available from the British Library

ISBN 9780224077873

The Random House Group Limited supports The Forest Stewardship
Council (FSC), the leading international forest certification organisation.
All our titles that are printed on Greenpeace approved FSC certified paper
carry the FSC logo. Our paper procurement policy can be found at
www.rbooks.co.uk/environment

Mixed Sources

Product group from well-managed
forests and other controlled sources
www.fsc.org Cert no. TT-COC-2139
© 1996 Forest Stewardship Council

Typeset in Bembo by Palimpsest Book Production Limited,
Grangemouth, Stirlingshire

Printed and bound in Great Britain by
CPI Mackays, Chatham, Kent ME5 8TD

CONTENTS

What Becomes   1

Wasps   23

Edinburgh   35

Saturday Teatime   55

Confectioner's Gold   73

Whole Family with Young Children
Devastated   91

As God Made Us   109

Marriage   125

Story of My Life   137

Sympathy   151

Another   177

Vanish   197

WHAT BECOMES

The cinema was tiny: twelve rows deep from the blacked-out wall and the shadowed doorway down to the empty screen, which had started to bother him now, a kind of hanging absence.

How did they make any money with a place this small? Even if it was packed?

Which it wasn't. Quite the reverse. There was, in fact, no one else here. Boy at the door had to turn the lights on just for him, Frank feeling bad about this, thinking he shouldn't insist on seeing a film all by himself and might as well go to the bigger space they kept upstairs which had a balcony and quite probably leg room and would be more in the way of a theatre and professional. In half an hour they'd be showing a comedy up there.

Or he could drive to a multiscreen effort: there'd been one in the last big town as he came round the coast – huge glass and metal tower, looked like a part of an airport: they'd have an audience, they'd have audiences to spare.

Although that was a guess and maybe the multiplex was empty, too. The bar, the stalls that sold reconstituted food, the toilets, the passageways, perhaps they were all deserted. Frank hoped so.

And he'd said nothing here as he'd taken back his torn stub and walked through the doorway, hadn't apologised or shown uncertainty. He'd only stepped inside what seemed a quietly watchful space as the younger man drifted away and left him to it.

Four seats across and then the aisle and then another four and that was it. The room wasn't much broader than his lounge and it put Frank in mind of a bus, some kind of wide, slow vehicle, sliding off towards destinations it left undisclosed.

He didn't choose a seat immediately, wandering a little, liking the solitude, a whole cinema of his own – the kind of thing a child might imagine, might enjoy. He believed he would move around later if no one else appeared, run amok just a touch and leave his phone turned on so he could answer it if anybody called.

Then behind him there came a grumble of male conversation, a blurry complaint about the cold and then a burst of laughter and the noise of feet – heavy steps approaching and a softer type of scuffling that faded to silence. Frank was willing to be certain that Softer-foot was the kid from the door: lax posture and dirty Converse All Stars with uneven wear – product of a careless home, an unsupportive environment – probably he'd padded in behind Frank again for some reason and then headed out to the foyer – that's how it sounded, but you never could tell.

At least one person was still there, still loitering, and for a moment this was almost unnerving. Frank being alone in a cinema, that was all right – alone in a muddle of people in a cinema, that was all right – just yourself and one other, two others, strangers at your back as the lights dim and the soundtrack starts to drown out everything – that might not be good. Silly to think that way, but he did.

For a moment.

Then he focused on being irritated, his nice privacy broken when it had extended so very far by now, right up to the black walls that melted when you studied them, disappeared down into the black carpet and left you adrift with nothing but the dull red shine of the seats and a sense of your skin, your movement, fidgets of life.

4

It was fine, though. Nobody joined him. The heavy steps withdrew, closed themselves up, Frank guessed, inside the projectionist's box, accompanied by a ruminative laugh. After that a regular, clattering slap started up and he supposed this to be the sound of loose film at the end of a reel, but he couldn't imagine why it was simply rattling round again and again.

He waited, the clatter persisting, his feet and fingers beginning to chill. One punter, apparently, didn't merit heating. Even if it wasn't logical to assume he'd be impervious.

He was still human and still here.

Little vents near the ceiling breathed and whispered occasionally, but that would be the wind outside disturbing them. The night was already roaring out there and set to turn worse, rain loping over the pavements, driven thick, and a bitterness underlying it that ached your teeth, your thinking. Warmth had drained from his shins where his trousers were soaked and the coat he was huddled into was only a fraction less damp.

Frank put on his hat.

The rattle of unattached film continued. And he believed he'd heard a chuckle, then a cough. Frank concentrated on his head which felt marginally warmer, because of the hat. Good hat: flat cap, proper tweed and not inexpensive. A man should have a hat, in his opinion. Beyond a certain age it will suit him and give him weight, become a welcome addition to his face, almost a trademark. People will look at his hat as it hangs on the back of a chair, or a coat hook, or rests on the edge of his desk and they will involuntarily assume – *Frank's here, then. That's his hat. Frank's old, familiar hat.* Through time, there will be a small transfer of emotion and people who are fond of him will also like his hat, will see something in it: the mark of his atmosphere, his style: and they'll be pleased.

His own transfers were largely negative. For example, he truly detested his travelling bag. This evening it would be waiting inside his hotel room, crouching by his bed like the guard dog in an unfamiliar house. It always was by his bed, no matter where he was sleeping, neatly packed for when he'd have to leave, fill it with his time and carry it the way he'd enjoy being carried, being lifted over every obstacle.

Never thought he would use it on his own account – the bag. Never thought he'd steal his days from everyone and run away.

Not his fault. He didn't want this. She forced his hand.

He'd been in the kitchen, preparing soup. Each Friday he'd make them both a big vegetable soup: beans, leaves, potatoes, celery, lentils, tomatoes, bits of pasta, seasonal additions, the best of whatever he found available. Every week it would be slightly different – less cabbage, some butternut squash, more tamarind paste – but the soup itself would be a steady feature. If he was at home that evening he would cook. It would be for her. It would be what he quietly thought of as an offering – *here I am and this is from me and a proof of me and a sign of reliable love.* She could open some wine, maybe, and watch him slice: the way he rocked the knife, setting a comfy rhythm, and then the onions and garlic would go on the heat to soften and the whole house would start to smell domestic and comforting and he would smile at her, tuck his ingredients into the pan, all stripped and diced, and add good stock.

He'd been in the kitchen, slicing, no one to watch. French knives, he had, sharp ones, well balanced, strong, a pleasure to work with, and she'd been late home so he'd started off without her. The blade had slipped. With squash you've got to be careful because it's always tough and can deflect you, slide you into an accident. But he hadn't been paying attention and so he'd got what he deserved.

He'd been in the kitchen alone. Funny how he didn't feel the pain until he saw the wound. Proximal phalanx, left ring finger, a gash that almost woke the bone. Blood.

He'd been in the kitchen and raised his hand, had made observations, considered his blood. It ran quickly to his wrist, gathered and then fell to the quarry tiles below, left large, symmetrically rounded drops indicative of low velocity and a perpendicular descent, and haloing every drop was a tiny flare of threads, of starring. The tiles were fairly smooth, but still confused his fluid into throwing out fine liquid spines. Glass would be better, holding his finger close over glass might give him perfect little circles: the blood, as it must, forming spheres when it left him and the width of each drop on impact being equal to each sphere's diameter. You could count on that.

He'd been in the kitchen, being with the blood. He'd allowed the drops to concentrate at his feet, to pool and spatter, patterns complicating patterns, beginning to look like an almost significant loss. Twenty drops or so for every millilitre and telling the story of someone standing, wounded, but not too severely and neither struggling nor in flight.

He'd been in the kitchen and laid his own trail to the French windows. Tiny splashes hazed a power point in the skirting board, dirtying its little plastic cover – white, the kind of thing you fit to stop a child from putting its fingers where they shouldn't be. No reason for the cover, of course, their household didn't need it – protection from a hazard they couldn't conjure, an impossibility.

He'd been in the kitchen marking the reflections with his blood. Then he'd paused for a few millilitres before he needed to swipe his whole arm back and forth in mid-air, blood hitting the dark glass of the doors in punctuated curves, the drops legging down before they dried, being distorted by motion, direction, gravity. He'd pumped his fist, then tried to cup his hand, catch some of his flow, then cast it off again, drive it over his ghost face and the night-time garden outside, the dim layers of wind-rocked shrubs, the scatter of drizzle, thinner and less interesting than blood. He'd thrown overarm, underarm, tried to get a kick out of his wrist until the hurt in his hand felt anxious, abused. Then he'd rubbed his knuckles wetly across his forehead before cradling them with his other palm, while his physiology performed as could be predicted, increased heart rate jerking out his loss, building up his body of evidence. Read the blood here and you'd see perhaps a blade that rose and fell, or the clash of victim and attacker: blows and fear and outrage, shock.

He'd been in the kitchen and she had come in. Never even heard her unlock the front door, nor any of the usual small combinations of noise as she dropped her bag and shed her coat, made her way along the corridor and then stood. He'd only noticed her when she spoke.

'Jesus Christ, Frank. What have you done. What the fuck are you doing.'

He'd turned to her and smiled, because he was glad to see her. 'I'm sorry, the soup's not ready. It'll be . . .' He'd glanced at the clock and calculated, so that she'd know how to plan her time – she might want a bath before they ate. 'It'll be about nine. Would you like a drink?' He could feel a distraction, a moisture some- where near his right eyebrow.

'What the fuck are you doing.'

He'd smiled again, which meant that he might have seemed sad for the second or two before, 'I know, but nine isn't too late.' He needed to apologise and uncover how she was feeling – that would help their evening go well. Time spent paying attention to people is never wasted. 'Unless you're really hungry. Are you really hungry?' Her hair had been ruffled, was perhaps damp – some intervention of bad weather between her leaving the car and reaching their doorstep had disturbed it. Skin paler than normal but with strong colour at her cheeks, as if she was cold. Her suit was the chocolatey one with this metallic-blue blouse, a combination which always struck him as odd but very lovely, 'You look tired.' It was the fit of the suit. So snug. It lay just where your hands would want to. 'Would you like a bath? There'll be time. Once it's ready, it doesn't spoil.' She'd kept her figure: was possibly even slimmer, brighter than when they'd first met. 'I got some organic celeriac, which was lucky.' He seemed slightly breathless for some reason and heavy in his arms.

'What if I'd brought someone back with me. What if they'd seen . . . you.'

'I didn't . . .' and this was when he'd remembered that his finger was really currently giving him grief, extremely painful. He'd felt confused. 'I didn't think you were bringing anyone.'

At which point she'd lifted up a small pot of thyme he kept growing near the sink and had thrown it towards his head and he'd bobbed down out of the way so it had broken against a wall behind him and then hit the tiles and broken again. Peat and brownish ceramic fragments were distributed more widely than you might think and the plant lay near his feet, roots showing from a knot of earth as if it were signalling distress. Thyme was quite hardy, though, he thought it would weather the upset and come through fine in the end.

'It's all right. I'll get it.' Frank wondering whether the pan and brush was in the storm porch or the cupboard underneath the stairs. 'It'll be fine.' He couldn't think where he'd seen them last.

'It's not all right. It won't be fine.' And she walked towards him, sometimes treading on his track, her shoes taking his bloodstains, repeating them until she stopped where she was close enough to reach up with her hand and brush his forehead, his left cheek, his lips. This meant his blood was on her fingers, Frank softly aware of this while she met his eyes, kept them in the way she used to when he'd just arrived back from a trip, a job – this was how she'd peered in at him then, seemed to be checking his mind, making sure he was still the man he'd been before.

After the look she'd slapped him. Fast. Both sides of his jaw. 'It's not all right.' Leaving and going upstairs. He didn't follow because he was distracted and he shook his head and ran his tongue along against his teeth and felt he might have to accept that he no longer was the man he'd been before.

Not that he'd been anybody special.

And this evening he was apparently even less: the sort of man who'd sit in a cinema but never be shown a film.

The projection box had quietened, the rattling stilled. There had been a few ill-defined thumps a while ago and then silence and the sensation of being watched. Frank was quite sure the projectionist had decided not to bother with the movie and was waiting for Frank to give up and go away.

But that wouldn't happen. Frank was going to get what he wanted and had paid for. Overhead, deep mumbles of amplified sound were leeching through the ceiling, so the other feature had begun. Still, he suspected that no one was watching upstairs, either – he'd not heard a soul in the foyer.

Half an hour, though – if the comedy had started, that meant he'd been stuck here for half an hour.

He removed his hat and then settled it back on again.

Being left for half an hour was disrespectful, irritating. Any longer and he would be justified in growing angry and then making his displeasure felt.

He coughed. He kicked one foot up on to the back of the chair in front, followed it with the other, crossed his legs at the ankle. He burrowed his shoulders deeper into the back of the seat. This was intended to suggest that he was fixed, in no hurry, willing to give matters all the time they'd take. The next step would involve conflict, tempers, variables it was difficult and unpleasant to predict.

Only then a motor whirred and the light dimmed further then dispersed and the screen shivered, jumped, presented a blurry certificate which adjusted to and fro before emerging in nice focus and showing him the title of his film, the entertainment he had picked. Silently, a logo swam out and displayed itself, was replaced by another and another. Silently, a landscape appeared and displayed itself, raw-looking heaps of brown leaves, blades of early mist between trees, quite attractive. Silently, the image altered, showed a man's face: an actor who'd been famous and attractive some decades ago and who specialised these days in butlers, ageing criminals, grandfathers, uncles. Silently, he was looking at a small girl and silently he moved his lips and failed to talk. He seemed to be trying to offer her advice, something important, life-saving, perhaps even that. But he had no sound.

The film had no sound. What Frank had, at first, thought was an artistic effect was, in fact, a mistake – perhaps a deliberate mistake.

He kept watching. Sometimes, when he'd been abroad, he'd gone to the cinema in foreign languages and managed to understand the rough flow of events. He'd been enter-tained well enough.

But this was an artistic piece, complicated. People seemed to be talking to each other a good deal and with a mainly unreadable calmness. As soon as the child dis-appeared, he was lost.

So he stood, let the chair's seat bang vaguely as it flipped out of his way, and strode up the incline of the invisible floor towards the invisible wall and its hidden doorway.

Outside, the projectionist's box was clearly labelled and

its door was, in any case, ajar, making it very easy to identify – an unattended projector purring away there, a dense push of colour and motion darting out through the small glass window in a bundle of shifting strands and rods that thinned as they spanned the cinema and then opened themselves against the screen. It was always so clearly defined: that fluttering, shafted light. Frank briefly wondered if the operator had to smoke, or scatter talc, raise steam to make sure it stayed that way, remained picturesque.

In the foyer, there was the boy with the dirty shoes, leaning against a pillar and looking drowsy.

'There's no sound.'

'What?'

'I said, there's no sound.'

The boy seemed to consider saying *what* again before something, perhaps Frank's expression, stopped him.

'I said, there's no sound.' Frank not enraged, not about to do anything, simply thinking – *no one helps and you ask and it doesn't matter because no one helps and I don't know why.* He tried again: 'I can't hear. In the normal way I *can* hear. But at the moment I can't. Not the film. Everything else, but not the film. That's how I know there's something wrong with the film and not with me.'

The boy was eyeing him, but didn't seem physically strong or apt to move abruptly.

Frank believed that he felt calm and was not being threatened. He continued to press his point. 'There is a problem with the film. The film is playing, but there's no sound.' And to explain what he'd been doing for all of this time. 'It's not been started long and it has no sound.' Although this maybe made him seem foolish because who would have normally waited more than half an hour in a cold, dark room for a film to start.

'There's no sound?' The boy's tone implied that Frank was demanding, unreasonable.

Frank decided that he would like to be both demanding and unreasonable. If he wasn't the man he had been, then surely he ought to be able to pick the man he would be. 'There's no sound.' Frank swallowed. 'I would like you to do something about it.'

This wasn't a tense situation, he'd thought it might be, but he'd been wrong. His potential opponent simply shrugged and told him, 'I'll go and find the projectionist.'

'Yes, you should do that.' Frank adding this unnecessarily because the boy had already turned and was dragging across the foyer carpet.

Something would be done, then.

Frank sat on the small island of seats provided, no doubt, for short periods of anticipation – people expecting to be joined by other people, parties assembling, outings, families, kids all excited by the prospect of big pictures, big noise, a secure and entertaining dark. The door to the larger auditorium was open and he could see a portion of the screen, the giant chin and mouth of a woman. There were also figures in some of the seats, filmgoers. Or models of filmgoers, although that was unlikely. They must have been stealthy, creeping in: or else they'd arrived before him, extremely early. Either way, he'd not heard them, not anticipated they'd be there.

That was surprising. Frank prided himself on his awareness and observation and didn't like to think they could fail him so completely. In a private capacity this would be alarming, but it would be disastrous in his work. He was resting at the moment, of course. Everybody who'd said that he ought to rest had been well intentioned and well informed. He'd needed a break. Still, there would come a day when he'd return and then he'd need his wits about him.

Expert. That's what he was.

'There are other things you can do.'

She hadn't understood. When you're an expert then you have an obligation, you must perform.

'There are other things to think about.'

She'd never known the rooms he'd seen: rooms with walls that were a dull red shine, streaking, hair and matter: floors dragged, pooled, thickened: footprints, hand prints, scrambling, meat and panic and spatter and clawing and smears and loss and fingernails and teeth and everything that a person is not, should not be, everything less than a whole and contented person.

Invisible rooms – that's what he made – he'd think and think until everything disappeared beyond what he needed: signs of intention, direction, position: the nakedness of wrong: who stood where, did what, how often, how fast, how hard, how ultimately completely without hope – what exactly became of them.

Invisible.

At which point, his mind broke, dropped to silence, the foyer around him becoming irrelevant. A numbness began at the centre of his head and then wormed out, filling him with this total lack of anything to hear. He tried retracing his thoughts but they parted, shredded, let him fall through into an undisclosed location. And the man he'd been before was gone from him absolutely, he could tell, and whatever was here now stayed suspended, thoughtless.

No way of telling how long. Not even enough to grip hold of and start a fear. Maybe mad. Maybe that's what he was. Broken or mad. Broken and mad.

Then in bled a whining: a thinner, more pathetic version of his voice and his mind seemed to catch at it, almost comforted.

No one helps.

It felt like a type of mild headache.

No one ever helps. I just stay at home and the light bulbs die and the ceilings crack and everything electrical is not exactly as it should be – there are many faults – and I call the helplines and they don't, I call all kinds of people and they don't help, I spend hours on the phone and I get no answers that have any meaning, I get no sense – there are constantly these things going wrong, incessantly, every day, and I want to stop them and I could stop them but no one helps and I can't manage on my own.

Like that evening with the blood – he couldn't very well have been expected to deal with those circumstances by himself.

He'd done all he could, waited in the kitchen and kept the soup on a low heat so that it would be ready for her. Except that wasn't the main point.

His finger was the more important detail. He washed that under the tap and then wound it round with an adhesive dressing from the first-aid kit. He'd used the kit in the hallway cupboard rather than go and maybe disturb her in the bathroom.

The bathroom, that was more important than his finger. He'd been guessing she was in the bathroom, because the hot water was running, he could tell from the boiler noise, and she'd probably been in there adding bath oil, enjoying the steam, getting the temperature right for steeping in – he hadn't known. He never had seen her bathing, the details.

The bathroom was connected with his finger because he'd bound his injury downstairs so as to avoid her and had possibly not done this well, maybe he should have taken better steps to close the wound, because the scar that he'd eventually grown was quite distinct. If anyone examined his hands closely they would see it – an identifying mark.

Then – a key point – he'd noticed that his shirt was bloody and he should change it and that had meant changing his plans and going upstairs, sneaking into their bedroom, pulling out any old sweater and wrestling it on.

The smell of her in the bedroom. Same thing you'd get when you hugged her, or rolled over on to her pillow when she wasn't there. Frank had seen men hug their wives, the way they'd fit their chin down over the woman's shoulder and there would be this smile, a particularly young-seeming expression with closed eyes – always made him think – *bliss.*

That one soft word, which in every other context he did not like or use.

Going up to the bedroom had been unwise – she might have been there, too, resting on her pillow, or undressing and having some kind of large emotion that she didn't want to be observed. But he'd been careful to listen at the bathroom door as he passed it and had heard the sound of her stirring in the bath, a rise and fall of water, some kind of smoothing motion.

Somehow, that was another point to emphasise. It should not be forgotten, that moment of leaning beside the door and listening to a movement he could not see and imagining his wife's shoulder, side of the breast glimpsed, her cheek, the lift of her ribs – always a slim girl – and a glimmer of water chasing over and down, being lost.

Once he'd put on his sweater, Frank thought he was hungry and so he'd gone down to the soup, cut into the bread he'd baked – a moist, yeasty loaf made with spelt, which was a little difficult to get, but worth the effort – and he'd ladled out some soup. When he took the first spoonful, though, it tasted salt, peculiar, and a lassitude in his arms and throat disturbed him and he ended up throwing his bowlful away.

It wasn't that he didn't realise she was upset.

He did know her and did understand.

She'd brought no one home and they had no children, no child, and she was the only person who'd seen him, just her, and they were married, had been married

for years, so that should have been all right. But her feelings did exist, of course, and should be considered. She
was upstairs bathing and having emotions. Undoubtedly
the most important thought that he could have, should
manage to have, would be that she had feelings. These
feelings meant she didn't like his soup, or his bread, or
his hat and she blamed him for terrible things, for one
terrible thing which had been an accident, an oversight,
a carelessness that lasted the space of a breath and meant
he lost as much as her, just precisely as much.

He wanted to go to her and say: *I've watched this before,
been near it – the way that a human being will drop and break
inside, their eyes dying first and then their face, a last raising
of light and then it goes from them, is fallen and won't come
back. They walk into our building and whatever they think
and whatever we have told them, there is a person in their
mind, a living, unharmed person they expect to greet them and
return their world. Then our attendants lead them to the special
room, to the echoing room, and they see nothing, no one, no
return, a shape of meat, an injury. Some of them cry, some
accept the quiet suggestion of tea and the plate of biscuits we
set down to make things seem homely and natural and as if
life is going on, because it is, that is what it does – picks us
up and feeds us with itself, drives us on until we wear away.
Some of them are quiet, inward. Some I can hear, even in my
office. They rage for their lovers, their loves, for their dead love,
their dead selves. And they rage for their children. And they
fail to accommodate their pain. And they leave us in the end,
because they cannot stay. They go outside and fall into existence.
Our town is full of people running back and forth in torn days
and every other town is like that, too. Our world is thick with
it, clotted in patterns and patterns of grief. And, beyond this, I
know you're sad. I know your days are bleeding, too. And
I know I make you sad. I don't understand how not to, but
please don't bring in more of the grief, don't add to it. If there
is more, then I won't be able to breathe and I'll die.*

And I miss her, too.

And I miss her like you do.

The no one who comes home with you holding your hand.

The girl who isn't there to mind when I hurt myself.

'That'll be okay, then.'

Frank saw the young man's sneakers, the intentionally bedraggled cuffs of his jeans. Frank looked at them through his fingers, keeping his head low. 'I'm sorry.' This emerging less as a question than a statement, a confession. He rubbed his neck, his helpless sweat, and said again, more clearly and correctly, 'I'm sorry?'

'The projectionist's just coming back. You can go in and wait.'

Oh, I know about that, I've done that. Wait. I can do that. Past master.

Frank swallowed while his anger crested and then sank. These spasms were never long-lasting, although they used to be less frequent. That could be a cause for concern, his increased capacity for hatred.

'Are you okay?'

The boy staring with what appeared to be mild distaste when Frank straightened himself and looked up. 'No. At least, yes. I am okay. I have a headache, that's all.'

Standing seemed to take an extremely long time, Frank trying not to fall or stagger as he pressed himself up through the heavy air. He was taller than the boy, ought to be able to dominate him, but instead Frank nodded, holding his cap in both hands – something imploring in this, something anachronistic and disturbing – and he cranked out one step and then another, jolted back to the doorway of the cinema and through.

The dark was a relief, peaceful. He felt smoother, healthier as soon as it wrapped him round, cuddled at his back and opened ahead to let him pad down the gentle slope and find a new seat.

It was actually good that his film had been delayed. This way, his evening would be eaten up − back to the hotel after and head straight for bed. Double bed. Only one of him. No need to pick a side: her side, his side. He could lie where he wanted.

She preferred the left. He'd supposed this was somehow to do with the bedroom door being on the right. Any threat would come in from the right and he would be set in place to meet it. Frank had thought she was letting him guard her while she slept: Frank who was perfectly happy on whatever side was left free, who might as well rest at the foot of the bed like a folded blanket. It didn't matter. He didn't mind.

Really, though, she didn't expect Frank to defend her. Her choice had nothing to do with him. In fact, they'd had other bedrooms with the door in other places and with windows that could be climbed through, you had to consider them, too − their current window was to the left − and she'd still always lain on the left. She liked that, or was used to it, or had given it some importance which couldn't be altered now. Her book, her water glass, they were left.

She hadn't read on their last night, at least he didn't think so. He'd waited for her in the kitchen with the soup and she'd never come down. He'd cleaned up his blood and repotted the plant and listened to the sound of the water draining from her bath and her naked footsteps on the landing, not moving towards the stairs. Then he'd decided his first cleaning hadn't been thorough and he'd scrubbed the place completely − work surfaces, floor, emptied out the fridge and wiped it down, made it tidy. The cupboards needed tidying, as well. That took quite a time. Finally, he decanted the rest of the soup into a container, washed the pot, looked at the container, emptied it into the bin and washed the container.

It was two in the morning when he was done.

And when he had slipped into bed he had expected her to be sleeping, because that would be best.

'What were you doing?' Only she wasn't asleep, she was just lying on her back without the light on and waiting to ask him, 'What were you doing?'

'I . . . cleaning.'

'What's wrong with you.'

And Frank couldn't tell her because he didn't know and so he just said, 'I understand why people look at fountains, or at the sea. Because those don't stop. The water moves and keeps on moving, the tide withdraws and then returns and it keeps on going and keeps on. It's like –' He could hear her shifting, feel her sitting up, but not reaching for him. 'It's like that button you get on stereos, on those little personal players – there's always the button that lets you repeat – not just the album, but the track, one single track. They've anticipated you'll want to repeat one track, over and over, so those three or four minutes can stay, you can keep that time steady in your head, roll it back, fold it back. They know you'll want that. I want that. Just three or four minutes that come back.' Which he'd been afraid of while he'd heard it and when he'd stopped speaking she was breathing peculiarly, loudly, unevenly, the way she would before she cried. So he'd started again, because he had no tolerance for that, not even the idea of that. 'I want a second, three, four seconds, that would be all. I want everything back. No stopping, I want nothing to stop.' Only he was crying now, too – no way to avoid it. 'I want her to be –' His sentence interrupted when she hit him, punched out at his chest and then a blow against his eye causing this burst of greyish colour and more pains and he'd caught her wrists eventually, almost fought her, the crown of her head banging against his chin, jarring him.

Afterwards they had rested, his head on her stomach, both of them still weeping, too loudly, too deeply, the din of it ripping something in his head. But even that had gone eventually, and there had been silence and he had tried to kiss her and she had not allowed it.

That was when he had taken his bag and left the room, the house, the town, the life.

I miss her, too.

Behind Frank, the projector stuttered and whirred, light springing to the screen and sound this time along with it. He fumbled into his pocket and found his phone, turned it off. That way he wouldn't know when it didn't ring, kept on not ringing.

Frank tipped back his head and watched the opening titles, the mist, the trees, the older man's face as it spoke to the small girl's, as he spoke to his daughter. And the world turned unreliable and lost him and the film reeled on and he knew that it would finish and knew that when it did he would want nothing more than to start it again.

WASPS

Their da going away again, that's all it was. Both boys saying nothing about it, but awake at five and thumping downstairs and straight out to the garden, Jimbo still wearing pyjamas and Sam in his yesterday's clothes, probably no pants – some objection he has at the moment to pants, as if they were practically nappies and grownups never wore them. The first fight beginning as soon as they left the house: she has a memory of dozing through whole cycles of shouts and squealing and that odd, flat roar Sam has started to produce whenever he truly abandons himself and just rages. No tantrums for Sam, not any more. He is seven now. He has the real thing. He has rage.

And the morning was out of its balance already, aggressive. Orange-pink light had been creeping forward and threatening by four, summer pushing everything earlier and earlier whether you wanted it to or not, and the bed too hot and what might be called a real gale had been rising outside until her sleep was full of its pressure against the corner of the house, air leaning so hard at the window glass that she felt breathless and unsettled, searched by a hunger that needed, that pried.

The house grew disturbed, doors pestering at their frames whenever the weather drew breath: clatters on the roof, something twisting, scouring overhead, and meanwhile she dreamed a little of being underwater, swimming the length of an assault course, both a game

and an assault course, in some kind of terrible amuse-
ment park. She was fully dressed, heavy, but doing her
best to thread a way along flooded passages, over ramps,
gasping up into sudden pockets of lovely air and then
driving herself back down to find this or that opening
into caves, or water-filled dining rooms, church halls, or
a place like a fishmonger's shop, except every fish in it
still alive – tethered by hooks through the bodies and
heads, fluttering by the white-tiled walls and hanging in
strings of blood, staring at her while she kicked and
wallowed past.

All the time, she'd kept thinking, 'I shan't bring the
children here, it seems unsafe. There must surely be
someone I could inform, a procedure to follow for
complaints. What I need is a higher authority – one I
would ask to set right.'

The logic of it mostly faded as she woke, but she had
been left with a definite shame, the embarrassed anticipation that she might drown, be lost somewhere in
the game when nobody else had a problem with it,
because it was, in fact, so simple and undemanding – like
a tunnel of love, or a ghost train, a romp round the
funhouse mirrors and then back to have your tea.

By the time she leaned round and looked at the alarm
it was getting on for half past seven, and the boys were
still noisy, loud against the weather. Which was how they
dealt with it – the leaving – by giving each other reasons
to cry and reasons to be angry. Their father was curled
on his side, hands tucked under his chin and offering
her that face, the one that always made her think he
wasn't sleeping, was only waiting with his eyes closed
until she had gone, or until something interesting
happened, a surprise. Although as a couple they weren't
much prone to surprises. Predictable, was Ray.

She dressed in a T-shirt and cardigan, what used to be
good jeans – as if she were someone who could be stylish,

but was presently relaxed – the weekend was when you relaxed – and then she went to the windowsill so she could check on the wasps. There always were wasps. Always dead – or else weak and sleepy, crawling off to a permanent halt behind the chest of drawers. Five today. All goners. As if the house drew them and then destroyed them. Ridiculously fragile wings, perfect stripes and tapered bodies, altogether finely worked – they were like very tiny toys. Of course, you quite naturally worried that somebody would barefoot on top of one by mistake. The boys not really at risk, though, because they were not allowed into Mummy and Daddy's bedroom. None of that letting the kids burrow in between their parents for the night – could ruin a marriage, nonsense like that. And the bed wasn't big enough for four. Not even three.

She cupped the wasps up in her hand, the window frame shuddering beside her as the storm sneaked in a draught to stir the dead wings, their stiffened weightlessness. She patted the glass, smiled and left the room and let the corridor draw her along, then the stairs, another corridor until she arrived in the kitchen, because she would forever and ever arrive in the kitchen – no will or effort necessary: there she would be in unironed clothes, nothing to show what was left of her shape – as scruffy as her children, an inadequate bloodline no doubt apparent in every fault the three of them displayed.

But no time for morbid reflection – she walked to the back door, opened it and called her sons, opened it and opened her palm, let the clean breeze take the wasps and make them gone.

And now.

Sunday today, so she made a proper breakfast: a nice hearty send-off for Ray. He'd be gone before lunch and who knew what he'd be eating while he was away.

Sausage, fried eggs, bacon, black pudding, toast *and* potato scones, ketchup, peanut butter, marmalade – enough to finally lure the boys into the kitchen on smell alone. As she could have guessed, they were not speaking: Jimbo tearful and Sam brooding, each of them, she knew, on the verge of telling her how badly they'd been treated by the other and how wrong everything was.

She decided to get in first, impose order. 'Wash your hands, they're horrible.'

'I can't.' Jimbo displaying a pretty much unscathed hand. 'Sam hit my thumb with a stone and made it bleed.' She settled her fingers on his forehead, felt the race of the storm still caught there: its lightness and its cold.

'He hit *me* all morning. He always hits me. And you always let him.' Sam washing his own hands thoroughly, theatrically, with the air of a weary surgeon. As she watched, the weight of an older brother's tribulations and sad duties hardens his jaw enough for him to look very much like his father. 'My foot is bleeding. But I never said.'

She offered him a plateful of everything, but failed to catch his eye, Sam having developed a habit of speaking to their floors. 'I never said anything.' He is growing increasingly oblique.

'Yes, well, you have said now.' It occurs to her that he'll be an appalling teenager. Quite possibly Ray was, too. 'He's much smaller than you and you mustn't hit him —' They maybe had bad genes on both sides, then, her poor boys.

'See!' Jimbo crowing this and grasping a piece of toast in his wounded, filthy hand.

'And you, little man, mustn't annoy him until he hits you. Sam is your brother and you have to take care of each other.'

'I hate him.'

'No, you don't. Wash your hands. *Now.* Don't put that toast back on the plate. We don't want it. Come and sit

down and join us, Sam. Jimbo, you do go and wash. I
mean it. And both of you behave. Da will be very upset
if the last thing he sees of you is two dirty boys who
can't be at peace. Let's have a good morning. Before your
mother starts to scream and doesn't stop and has to be
taken away to the hospital for screaming people. Who
would make your breakfasts then?'

Her sons showed no sign of having heard her and she
wondered again which of her threats they would
remember, which would be useful and which would scar.
It never was easy to tell, she supposed, if your parenting
was mostly beneficial, or bound to harm.

Ray, there was something in Ray which was nearly
dangerous. She'd found him with Jimbo last night – the
child with his hair curled and damp from the bath, clean
pyjamas, the face she strokes without thinking, cups with
her palm while she stands behind him and he leans his
shoulders back on her knees and she finds the narrow
jolts of his vertebrae, rubs them up and down for luck,
reassurance, delight. (She does the same with Sam when
he'll let her, has no favourite. They are her two boys.
Inescapable. Irreplaceable. Inescapable.) His father was
sitting beside him on the bed, Jimbo's chest rising and
sagging with too hard, too uneven breaths, showing every
sign of wanting to run up into a crying bout, a full-
blown, wailing fit of it.

But Ray had blocked him, snapped him to a stop. 'You
wouldn't want to have no food, would you? Or no house?
And none of your things. Juggy the bear over there . . .'

'He's not a bear.' Jimbo using his smallest voice, the
one to make you think he was still much younger.

'Well, Juggy, anyway – there would have been no money
to buy him if I didn't go off and work. Your mother
doesn't earn any money, she just works here. So I give
her money and she spends some of that on you and *I*
spend money on you and . . .' He'd smiled as if he'd just

worked out something important and complicated and now he could show it off. 'Your brother and you are both very expensive.' Ray lifted Jimbo's chin with his finger so that he could concentrate on the boy's eyes: the soft, large target they made. 'Would you want to be a homeless boy with nothing?'

Jimbo with no answer to this.

'Would you want to be cold and hungry?'

Again there was no possible reply.

And she wanted to feel this kind of bullying might simply be what males did with each other – men with men, men with boys, boys among themselves. She aimed for the hope that it was natural, normal, a minor way of hardening the heart against later misfortunes.

'That's why I go away, Jimbo. For you.'

Something in Jimbo, she could tell, decided then that his father left him, because of his needing toys and wanting to play with Juggy. Jimbo's hurt was delicately, irrevocably becoming Jimbo's fault while she watched: there it went, slipping, stealing in. Another year or so and he'd have noticed what Sam has already figured out – that love and pain are names for the same thing. Give one, mean the other. Get one, want the other. Mean one, get the other back for it. Want one, want the other, want both.

'Don't tell them that.' She'd had to mention it in the evening. Although she was all for a quiet life – still, it wasn't right, to fortify the heart by killing it. 'I said, don't tell them that – don't make it seem like their fault that you go away.'

'Well, it's true.'

'Then particularly don't say it to them.'

Ray looked out of the bedroom window, tilted his chin, opened his mouth just a touch and tapped his finger-nail against his bottom teeth. This meant he wouldn't answer.

She changed direction. 'What are you going to do about the wasps . . .' And that sounded like nagging, when she absolutely didn't want to nag – this their last night – last night together before he's off – the two of them making the memory he'll take with him. 'I mean, they're still coming in. It's odd.'

'Mm.' He rubbed hard at his hair, made it stay lifted, disordered, so that when his hand fell he seemed softer, seemed perfectly and precisely lovable. He turned to her. 'I'm sorry – What?' His expression was polite. Yes, that was the word for it – polite. 'Wasps . . .'

'Yes.'

'Well, I did check. You saw me. I checked. And there wasn't a nest, a colony, something like that. Not anywhere near. There was nothing.'

'I wondered where they come from, that's all.'

'They're getting in through a closed window – that's what I don't understand. All shut up tight, but still they get in at me. It shouldn't be possible.'

'But it is.'

And this the point where it had happened again – *still they get in at me* – a safe conversation becoming unwieldy, changing its face. She'd tried not to consider if he thought this when he met the women, when he first saw in them whatever it was that he needed, wanted, and began the process, the arrangements, the exchanges he found necessary. Did he look at them and decide, was there hesitation, wonderment? – *still they get in at me.*

Ray had grinned at her, winked. 'Never mind the wasps, though. Let's say goodbye.'

'Goodbye.' His right to make this mean hardly anything, or everything – *goodbyegoodbyegoodbye* – and her right to not know.

'You know what I mean.'

When she does not.

His grin wider. 'You do know.' It touches her, cold on her forehead and in her hair, lifting.

He'd extended his arms, very tender, easy, warm – the husband who wants to hug his wife and then take her to bed and croon damp words in her ear, small encouragements, as if she were an animal in need of guidance, maybe liable to shy away at the more demanding drops and slopes and jumps. 'Come on, love. It'll all be okay.'

And she did step in, did almost tumble towards him – his long arms wrapping round her, friendly.

'Hello.' Cheery, he'd sounded.

She hadn't answered, not being especially cheery herself.

Now she waited for him in the kitchen as the boys hacked at their food and took too much ketchup because they could tell when she wasn't paying enough attention to make them stop. In the garden, wind was clawing at the flowers, breaking things, the trees wild with it beyond the fence.

'All right, then.' Behind her, Ray was standing, very neat. She shifted her chair round and saw the business suit – which she'd expected – and the coat – which wasn't entirely unanticipated, either. He was already wearing his coat. He never did like hanging around. Sam understood the situation as quickly as she did, shoving his chair back and rushing to hold his father's legs. Jimbo followed, but was more hesitant – as if he might have the power to carelessly make something worse.

'You're not going yet.' Sam muffled, his face pressed hard to Ray's trench coat. 'Too soon.'

She heard herself having to ask, 'Yes, couldn't you eat something? With us?'

'Sorry.' He took hold of his children's collars and began to tug them back and forth, play-fighting, casual strength in the thin forearms, wiry cunning. The boys squealed and he shook them more, going slightly too hard at it, the way that he usually did, until their faces were still pleased, but their eyes were very mildly afraid.

Ray shrugged at her. 'Slept in. You should have woken me. I'll be racing all the way now.' He glanced down at Sam and Jimbo. 'Racing . . . yes I will be . . .' His own eyes comfortable, ready to see other faces, other people.

She cannot tell him, because they have resolved this issue, 'You should have let them be with you longer. You know how they'll get, once you've left. Actually, no, you don't – you're not here.'

She cannot suggest, because this would be picking a fight, 'I do believe that you still love me and I would have thought that would be the most important thing, but in fact you no longer respect me and that is the worst, is the very worst. You love me, but I do not matter.'

She cannot say, because they have agreed this would be manipulative and inexcusable, 'This doesn't work. You can't keep telling me about the women, because this doesn't work. You can't say that I'm happy with your money and the house and that it's easier for me this way and I get to stay with the children and everything is familiar and stable and fine and you'll always come home and you'll never stay, but you'll always come home, but you'll never stay and I am here doing many, many things for which I do not respect myself. And you want impossible things and I can't do them.'

She does say, 'Well, if you have to go.' A draught from somewhere touches her face.

He nods, agreeing. 'Come on, then.' Hustling the boys along with him up the passage and half turned so that he can see her, reassure, 'I'll call you.' She stands, follows.

The door swipes open against him when he unlocks it, bangs Jimbo on his head so that he starts crying, howling. The hall full of weather.

'No damage done, brave lad. Gotta go. Bye now.'

Ray kisses Sam's forehead and reaches down for Jimbo, but the boy pulls away, runs to her and grabs her sweatshirt.

She has to fight her son's weight to reach the door, set a hand on Sam's shoulder, accept the brief squeeze of her arm that her husband leaves her.

Ray stands clear of them all on the path for a moment and waves, then spins, leans forward to the storm. It buffets him, live in his hair, punches his tie against his face, slaps under his coat and she watches him struggle and thinks this is how it should start – the timely intervention of some higher authority: the real force of everything: the rage. The coming rain should swing down like a blade while the storm takes him high and sets him right by shaking him apart.

She stands on the doorstep preparing herself. This is a way to be ready when he finally doesn't come back.

EDINBURGH

Peter's back was sore, maybe from lifting potatoes – not the big sacks, you prepared yourself for them and bent your knees the way you should, did what the Health and Safety poster told you. But there were little sacks, too – heritage varieties with comforting names and credentials from the Soil Association – and you'd take them in your stride, not thinking: two or three to either hand so you could fill up your display, and you'd be careless and you'd do yourself in. That's what always knackered you, lack of foresight.

Although today that wasn't fair, because the potatoes had done him no harm.

Peter dodged behind the counter and rang up three sharon fruit and a packet of energising tea for a man he vaguely recognised.

Doesn't even say 'Hello' though, or 'Good morning' or 'Thanks for not shoving your thumb into one of my sharon fruit while I'm distracted by fishing out a ten-pound note.' Fat wallet and a very crisp tenner – as if someone's starched it for him – good haircut, nice jacket – not really a shopper: more like a man who is pissing about in a break away from work. The sharon fruit will rot in the bag and he'll never drink the tea, because he's not healthy at heart. Bet his wife buys the food and keeps house, irons all his money. His wife, or his girlfriend. Maybe both.

Peter gave his customer a plastic bag that wouldn't be recycled, because said customer was a cunt, the sort of cunt who's barely aware of you, because you do not matter and who does not say goodbye.

Cunt.

Really.

It's a harsh word, but the only one that fits.

At the back of his shop there was a cork board shaggy with leaflets that advertised books about Spirit Guides and retreats that would heal you with horses and every other sort of shite. Sell organic food and imitation bacon and suddenly folk thought you'd tolerate anything. Poorly looking lunatics would rush at you from miles around with news of whatever had saved them from themselves.

I haven't got an Inner Child, I'd have known it by now if I did. Likewise with the Spirit Animals – I am not playing host to some interior bloody zoo. And a Spinning Trance would not bring me insight and Reiki would not make me glad. Reiki – that's the one where someone thinks about touching you and you think about it too and then you presumably both *have to keep thinking that all your thinking isn't an utter waste of time. It's like paying an electrician for thinking he might fix your lights.*

A man with patchy hair loss and no shame had turned up yesterday with a poster about seeing angels. Peter did not wish to live in a world where tutors could help you learn how to see angels – not even during a weekend of supportive workshops engendering an atmosphere of loving fellowship and with a former Buddhist monk on hand.

I don't want to see angels. How fucking terrified would you be, if you ever did?

Not that he'd object to being healthy, not at all. He'd lost weight lately, for example – was looking scrawny, sparse. But that was to do with boredom, or mango fatigue, or something else – it certainly wasn't a sign of disease. He didn't really eat much, that was the problem.

Trapped with fruit and vegetables for hours every working day, it wasn't fair to expect he should then go home and cook them, force them down. All of that peeling and cutting and fussing and boiling and chewing and swallowing, it was too much. So now he just bought this powdered stuff and drank it.

The pack says it's delicious and can be enjoyed at many different times. I have certainly tried it at many different times. I'm not sure I could pinpoint the truly enjoyable ones. I would allow that the range of flavours is impressive – but normal human beings could only be expected to tolerate three: Strawberry, Nothing and Chicken. I think Nothing's my favourite.

His powders did the job. And they contained chromium chloride and sodium molybdate, phosphorous, iodine, biotin: numerous arcane materials upon which he was apparently meant to thrive.

I may have been undernourished previously.

At lunchtime Peter whisked up his lunch in his personal mug with his personal fork and then drank it in the basement, because if you own the shop you can choose not to man the till at busy times and you should be able to stay undisturbed and chilly for the whole of your break if you want. It always was chilly in here – that was its disadvantage as a hiding place.

Fintan gangled down the steps at twenty past one. His trainers and jeans, emerging before him through the trapdoor, were even more paint-stained than usual which would mean that he'd been creating all night – probably some kind of sci-fi tableau – his descriptions of them generally sounded ghastly. He was laughing.

'What?'

'What?' Fintan seeming slightly alarmed when Peter stood up from among the boxes and pallets of stock.

'I said *what*. What are you laughing at?'

'Oh, yes . . .' Fintan paused and it was clear that he'd

come down intending to talk to someone who wasn't Peter.

'You were looking for Tim.'

'Yes.' He scratched under his two T-shirts, giving a glimpse of gingerish belly fur.

'He's not on yet. What were you laughing about?'

Fintan surrendered, because presumably any audience would do. 'I was out straightening up the display outside?'

Peter hated this – the way people made statements now as if they were questions, as if there was nothing definitive any more. It was American habit, or Australian. *It's bloody stupid, is what it is.*

'Yes, you were out with the display . . .'

Fintan rubbed the grubby-looking area within which he was trying to summon up a moustache. 'Right . . . and this old lady comes along? And she picks up a box of strawberries and she's tugging my sleeve and I'm wanting her to let me alone, because I thought she was complaining, but she wasn't.' Fintan grinned.

'And what *was* she? Having a heart attack? Propositioning you?'

'She wanted to know what to do with strawberries?'

'*What?*'

'She wanted to know what to do with strawberries. I mean, she was four hundred years old and she didn't know what to do with them and there's not much you *can*, like – is there? – add cream and sugar, or you make jam? So I'm listing stuff . . . strawberry crumble, strawberry pie, strawberry gravy, strawberry pudding, fricasse of strawberry risotto. Just this big fucking list and she's, like, just listening to it? Absolutely.'

This was Fintan who interfered with sharon fruit. Which was to say that all the assistants did and had and quite probably would – once one of them discovered the secret, you couldn't contain it. The knowledge that pressing your finger, pushing it in through the skin of a sharon fruit, felt so much, and so plainly, exactly like fingering something else that no young, hairy, grubby fruiterer could resist it – that wisdom could not be suppressed.

They used to be called persimmons, not sharons. Give them a chav name, this is what happens – they're easy – they'll let anyone have them, any time.

Fintan was still talking. 'Why do they pick me? There was another weirdy earlier – *which of these oranges will be the sweetest?* I just pointed – random . . . Why not?' He stretched. 'That's . . . and, anyway, how could you live that long and not know what to do with a strawberry for Christ's sake?'

'Maybe she was senile.'

'Yeah . . . I fucking hate them all.' Fintan hiccoughed a final giggle and then ducked and scrambled back up to the shop.

Peter went and put on the kettle, washed out his mug at the sink in what was supposed to be their earth-free area.

Bloody, bloody hell and damnation, I employ savages.

Because they don't bother me and they're cheap.

It occurred to him that the woman might simply have wanted company, a chat. If you were lonely enough, you might do that.

Because you'd want to change. People can change.

And, talking of change, my wallet has to go: I've had enough of it. You can't have a brown wallet – it's not right – and mine isn't even brown, it's beige. Why would anyone make beige leather? Can't have respect for yourself when you're dealing with that every day.

It was badly designed, in any case, I should have noticed when I bought it. Not enough places for all of the cards you're meant to carry so that you can drive your car and borrow books and rent out videos and pay by cheque and leave your parts to strangers when you're dead.

But it does give you this stupid, little pocket that wouldn't fit anything useful – when they designed it, what did they think? 'We'll have to provide them with somewhere to store three pence in coppers, or a lock of hair, some pepper.' And there's space for a photograph, only it's fronted with mesh, a black mesh, so if you put a picture in there, your sweetheart, or whoever, would be staring at you through a fog. She would be like a prisoner, like someone who couldn't see you at all.

But by two thirty it was venomously raining and Pete couldn't bring himself to leave the shop, never mind search out purveyors of quality wallets. So he replenished the mangoes – they were high-maintenance, mangoes – and the navel oranges and gave someone young a student discount, although she had no proper identification.

Probably has a cheap wallet – no room for her student card.

And they all come here for discounts, anyway: pensioner discount, staff discount, pal of staff discount, fancied by staff discount.

Not that it mattered. Flowers were what made the money. He could give the rest of it away, if he wanted – as long as Moira was lurking and tying bouquets and getting the love-sick to pay through the nose for carnations, or orchids, or roses: the floral cliché of their choice.

It's the thought that counts.

But people like thoughts demonstrated.

A twinge kicked in about his kidneys, perhaps a muscle out of sorts, but he felt he should keep on working at the till, because it formed a good distraction and there was nothing worse for pain than brooding.

Love-sick.

Love-sickened.

Love-sickness.

There's bound to be a workshop you can take for that.

Or you could simply stand in your shop and hear yourself dying and do the job that is supposed to pass your time – and then see her.

His day – that day – had not been ready for seeing her. His days were not ambitious in that way.

Other customers had been about because it was lunchtime, but they were just the usual. She wasn't. She was made of something different.

Silly, how you went home and you thought about her, having nothing else to occupy you beyond a small number of television programmes about Hitler and sharks, anything else being really too much of a challenge, if not an insult, to the mind.

'They ought to combine them. "Hitler's Sharks" – everybody would watch that.'

Your voice higher than it should have been, because of your thinned blood – she was thinning your blood – and this was the tenth, the eleventh time, that she'd been in – buying apples, russet apples – and, for some reason, she was late, not with you at half past one – as had become the custom – more like almost half past five which is when you close. The place is already empty – no last-minute death race for parsnips – Fintan mooching in the basement, doing God knows what, and so there is only you and her together and you're talking.

To be more precise, she is talking. 'It doesn't really matter what's on, I just go to sleep, anyway. Nine o'clock and I'm in my bed. That's dreadful, isn't it.' She is on her way home and wearing the striped scarf she always does – stripes along the length and not the width – and you know that her hair is soft, although you haven't touched it: you've memorised it – tumbled by the weather when she comes in and threads of light through it, mixed with the brown – and she has the type of fur-edged, padded coat that suggests she feels the cold and she is called Amanda and isn't uncomfortable telling you that and she knows that you are Peter, she knows you, and there is nothing dreadful, there could never be anything dreadful, about her being in her bed.

'Not as dreadful as trained Nazi sharks preying on merchant shipping and holding our plucky island race to ransom.' And you are adrift with her and racing, 'Do you know we're just about to . . . ? Is that all you . . . ? Because at half past five . . . ?' And down in the basement Fintan is having manual sex with fruit, is feeling fruit, 'The apples . . . ?' And with you, there is nothing definitive any more.

'They're what I want, yes.'

'Well, you just have them. They're going off. That is, they're fine to eat, they'll be fine for days. But everything's going off in the end, isn't it?'

All of which, amazingly, doesn't make her punch you and run away. She only takes the apples and puts them in her backpack. She doesn't leave you. 'Russets are nice, aren't they?'

You nod. 'A fine apple. 'Course, if I could get Adams Pearmain, I'd give you them.'

She only smiles and doesn't ask why and that means you don't get to tell her they are the best apples in the world, but still your progress with her is almost too unimpeded, topples you in your head – the way you're being with her and her with you: the way it makes you laugh and heats your hands, your chest – and she is younger than you, you're not sure by how much, but she's younger.

Maybe she's looking at you and thinking that you're older and believing that's a nice thing, as nice as apples.

'Fintan! Lock up, will you?' You are not feeling the cold. 'I'll walk you out, if you'd like.' You could be in your shirtsleeves, letting it snow, and still come to no harm. 'And wash your hands, Fintan!'

'You don't have to.' She smiles. 'You don't have to come with me.'

'No, I could do with some air. Very difficult to breathe in here – cigar smoke. It's the broccoli – they all smoke. I confiscate their matches, but they just get more – I

44

think from the cauliflowers – they are related, after all.' And, already beyond your control, your mouth says, 'D'you know, I could do with a coffee, too.'

This making her take your wrist, slightly clumsy. She squeezes your wrist, so that the shop hangs for a moment, lifted in hope. Then, 'I can't tonight,' before she lets you go.

'Oh.'

'Next time. If you're here.'

'Oh.'

Your upper arms unmanageable while you shrug at her, wordless, and then shepherd her out and along the street, because that seems correct – because of this frailty you find in her, a body that ought to be cared for.

For a while you do not notice you are shivering.

She points up ahead. 'I just catch the underground.' Small hands that seem calm. 'And then it's the train and then I walk back.'

This unfolds and tears in your stomach. 'Because you live . . . ?' The street dark with autumn.

'In Edinburgh.'

Mildly distant. 'Right.' But not impossibly so. 'I see.' The glow from the sign for the underground already visible. 'Hell of a journey . . .' And your head already keen to suggest that she should move closer, that this would be sensible, that you should have some say in where she lives.

'I know. Commuting . . . But I'm getting used to it. I have a good job here, a good flat there. Not good as if they're impressive, or anything, just good because I like them.' Lovely that she's shy like this, self-effacing. 'It means I read a lot, too – coming in, going back. I haven't got through this many books since I was a teenager.'

There had been a small kiss when they parted and no more shivering, his temperature fixed.

Got back and Fintan hadn't even noticed I'd been gone. Empty upstairs and I'd left the door unlocked – could have been robbed blind.

But I wasn't entirely *stupid – I just endangered my business for a while: I didn't blunder off into expecting that Amanda would let something happen, not between us, not really.*

I wasn't entirely stupid. Only happy.

Which is beyond stupidity, beyond any capacity for thought.

Peter banged the till hard enough to hurt his hand, brought himself back to here and now. This attracted Tim, a little concerned. 'Yes, chief?' Tim with the currently crimson sideburns and the succession of threatening T-shirts.

Makes me sound as if I'm running a fire station. Or a tribe. The greengrocer's tribe – any excuse for dancing round the spuds . . . Lordy, all the high jinks and madcap antics we enjoy.

'Look, I'm going to split some swedes in the basement. You take over.' Peter darting off to the back of the shop and down the stairs, because otherwise he'd have to suffer Tim's sympathetic expression.

Being pitied by a colour-blind twenty-year-old: precisely what I do not need.

What he did need was the cleaver and a good sack of swedes to halve and quarter, pretending this rendered them manageable and handy for single people, when in fact it just prevented him punching walls.

No one eats swede, anyway: it's old-fashioned.

He cleaved with unnecessary force.

He wrapped the first four slices in plastic.

He took another swede and cracked it, released that vaguely rancid scent.

He realised once again that the act of slicing was always less helpful than he hoped.

I never can split open the right thing.

His shoulders were starting to rise and clench – you had to watch that or you'd get these atrocious headaches.

I wasn't entirely stupid.

The boys, Tim in particular, had made more of matters than they should. Whenever Amanda arrived they would scurry off like schoolgirls. Or if Peter was stuck in the basement, they'd trot and fetch him and no pretence left that she was here for apples, for any kind of shopping.

Not that Pete was often downstairs, because she'd eased into the new habit of arriving at something past five and this became something he watched for, maybe once or twice a week, his vertebrae crouching in him until she appeared and he could leave with her and go to the coffee shop – the one with the filthy coffee, but at least it stayed open late – and they'd talk about books.

Nothing else.

She gave him books.

The same words that were in her mind, now in yours, still warm.

Books that seemed to indicate she knew him and what he would like.

Started off neutral: DeLillo, Jim Thompson: then Flann O'Brien, so you'd get a laugh. Then the James M. Cain: desperadoes and speed and sex. And sex.

He'd wanted to reciprocate. She'd never done the Russians, so he gave her *Anna Karenina* – all that love and honour and theories about The Land – and he'd gone out and bought lots of Chekhov so that she could have it. Chekhov who married late.

Older men and younger women. Very nineteenth century.

He celebrated with delighted complaints. 'You give me too much.' And this was true – she did.

'I have too many books.' She was looking at him.

'Got me reading again.'

'You've got me eating more fruit.' She was looking at him in a way that changed his face, made him different.

'So you'll live longer, which is good.'

'You'll live a long time, too. I insist.' She was looking

at him and making him loved – which is every difference in the world.

And she gave him R. Crumb – big book of his cartoons:
bits of philosophy and Catholic schoolgirls with monster
tits and fucking: people fucking guiltily, people fucking
freely, people fucking anything.

Looking at drawings of cocks that she must have looked at.

*Looking at a scrawny, naked man, caught in a box, twisting
and struggling in this tiny box, his soft, little dick lolling down,
defeated.*

You never know what someone means to send you.

And she lent him a fat hardback, an anthology of
poems – poetry not quite his thing – but he took it
home and waited until bedtime, had a shower and cocoa
to get comfy and then slipped down snug into bed and
opened up.

It was all right. Not fantastic. But all right.

*Stuff about buildings, deer, a broken window, dead relatives,
love.*

And then he was parting page 26 from page 27 and
there was a hair.

Hers.

Goldenish with little kinks in it and curved across the
paper.

He touched it.

Long enough to stretch from the tip of his middle
finger to the tenderest place in his wrist.

It touched him back.

He felt goldenish and afraid.

*Because it's always better to be contented than in love. But
when you've had nothing for so long, you get greedy and
confused. You want to be more than contented, you want to be
burned up alive and made again. You want always to have a
loved face.*

Why wouldn't you want that?

He didn't think he'd altered in the way he was with

her after that. It had only made more sense that he should start taking the train to Edinburgh at weekends, going to see her – and sharing new coffee shops, new books: the cold, malty air and the drizzle letting her soak into him, his clothes. They went to the big new cinema and held hands and giggled, but still kept holding. They took their pictures in the photo booth at the railway station.

In my wallet: her hair just cut and we wanted to immortalise it – this haircut – and her lips are quite thin but they have this delicacy and it seems she's about to speak or smile, and she was looking at me, letting me have the way that she looked at me.

In my wallet.

With me.

Need a new wallet now.

'You all right, chief?' Tim peered down the stairs, still seeming concerned, attentive, which was an irritation.

'Yes.'

'You, ah . . .' He crept a few steps lower. 'You're . . .' He pointed, apparently embarrassed by something that Peter had done, or else something he was.

And Pete glanced down, realised his thumb was bleeding, a chip cut into it, not too deep, but messy. 'Bollocks.' He'd have to sterilise the cutting surface, throw out the swedes.

'I can clean up, if you want.' Tim saying this, as if he's facing an invalid. 'You could just . . . you know. Wash your hand.'

Peter paused, blood dripping.

I am an invalid. Tim, Fintan, everybody: they saw me be well, be with her. They saw me burning.

Now all we do is remember what I'm not.

I should sack them.

His thumb only started hurting when he noticed it, once he understood what had gone wrong.

'I'll . . . Yes.' Peter finally moved to the muddy sink and the first-aid kit. 'If you could clean up. Yes.'

He ran the cold tap over his thumb, washed and washed, the water staying slightly pink, no matter what.

Party.

She'd been going to a party – somebody's birthday in a pub – and we'd never done something like that, been together in front of her friends.

Saturday evening in Edinburgh and you bring her flowers on the train, mind them for the whole of the journey so they're still nice.

Handing them over and she's on her doorstep and wearing make-up – night-out kind of make-up and this thin dress, silky, because it's summer, and she's still in stocking feet. Maybe tights – you don't know yet – but that's not how you say it – you say stocking feet, that's the accepted phrase. Her flat is behind her and you do not know it well, because you never can quite get a grip of it, because of watching her and gladly suffering the way the kitchen tabletop hurts a little under your hands, being covered in her using it and having breakfast and sitting at it to maybe read a book.

You wanted to sit a while, too, but she was smiling at the flowers and hurrying them into a sink full of water because she couldn't find a vase and then she's searching for her shoes without you and you're looking at her bookshelves and you mainly would like to just stay here and not go out and maybe your jeans aren't right and your shirt is silly, too young, but she takes your arm and kisses your cheek and that's the taxi sounding its horn in the street.

The pub is in a basement, lots of woodwork, bare stone and leather sofas: the heat in it already a bit much. Out at the back, there's a kind of garden and you fix yourself up there with drinks for both of you and she goes about and says hello to her pals and the birthday girl. That doesn't take long.

You meet three or four of her friends – four of them – and they seem pleasant and not surprised by you and she pats your arm while one of them is watching.

Peter dabbed his hand dry, fumbled out some anti-septic ointment and a plaster. Tricky to do a proper job with his hands unsteady.

It hadn't been a bad evening. A bit dull when they talked about places you hadn't been to, a past you didn't know. But then they mentioned Amanda's school, what she'd been like as a girl and that made her blush and unfurled the sum of you, rocked you.

And you missed the third-last train and the second-last and then you have to let out the five words boiling in your chest, 'I won't be going home.' You were quiet, but she heard you.

'No, Peter. You will be going home.' And her grin came a breath too late to stop me shivering.

Blood made a small stain through the dressing, as soon as he set it on straight. Small – nothing bad.

And you said, you truly said, you let yourself say, 'Well, I could get the bus. There's a later bus that goes to Glasgow, isn't there?'

But then you saw her, all over again saw her, like a new first time.

'No. You're going home to mine.'

In a whisper.

Like she's slapped you.

Whisper that runs down your neck and you're puzzled, you're knocked, you're split – there's this wonder yelling in you and all the outside of your face can do is frown, stare while she moves off into the room.

'No. You're going home to mine.'

She told me that and went away.

Saying goodbye.

She did a lot of hugging. I saw. And eventually she came and got me.

Leaving together. Thick and friendly and curious air around us, we pair.

*There's more hugging just as we go – strangers also hugging
me, because I am with her – and then we walk – Amanda in
heels, but she wants the air she says, she can make it as far as
we need to. Just that far.*
  A little bit drunk. Both of us.
  And we go.
  We take me home.
  We go home.
  *Only a few bright windows as we pass: high, grey, empty
streets.*
  *And I can't remember, but I do, and I won't remember, but
I do. Her hands on my back, as if she was listening to me,
reading.*
  Holding each other so much we could hardly undress.
  Her eyes closed.
  Stockings, not tights.
  Flat stomach.
  Goldenish cunt.
  Sweet word and it fits.
  He squeezed the place where the bloodstain was, did
it again, started climbing the stairs. A part of him hoped
that he might faint soon.
  Fits the line and shape and promise of all my life.
  All my fucking life.
  Up in the shop it was quiet, almost closing time – the
final half-hour when the ceiling would slowly grind down
towards Peter and his skull would throb.
  You slept for a while, but then woke without knowing why.
  *Amanda sitting on the edge of the bed and her skin cold,
shuddering, makes you flinch when you move to touch her. So
you wrap her up tight with you there in the sheet.*
  *Wanting to fuck her again, reaching round to her breast, but
it's sleeping, the nipple stays dull and her back is hard against
you, unhappy.*
  She'd begun with, 'I'm sorry.' Which is not a good
beginning, but he'd tried to welcome it.

'That's all right. I don't mind.' He'd been holding her hand, kissing it. 'But what's —'

She'd shaken her head and worked away from him and this took the rest of his sentence.

'I'm sorry.' Although she didn't sound it — was more bitter, perhaps, angry, his thinking panicked across possibilities.

'There's no need to be sorry.'

'I do care about you. I think about you all the time.'

Already the silt in your blood, the closing down.

'There was somebody at the party that I knew. That we used to . . . And I hugged him goodbye.'

Trying not to understand her. Trying hard.

'I . . . when we came back, I could still . . . I'm sorry . . . I could smell him on my clothes, on me — and then while we . . . it was like it was him.'

I think about you all the time.

'I do care about you.' And she'd brushed his back.

And I do love you.

'I just . . . this is a, this is a mess. I'm not what you . . . I don't want to hurt you.'

But you did.

'I don't think we can.'

But you fucking did.

'Could we just leave it for now.'

You fucking did.

Dressing himself had been difficult, because of his numbed hands. 'I'll call you. To see how you are.' Death starting with the hands.

His fingers delicate as ash.

A woman came into the shop: social worker type and wanting to talk when it's time to close, when it's time to give up and go away. She had leaflets.

'It works on the principles that all life is connected and this energy, it goes between us, there's a flow.'

Knitted hat, shoes made from recycled tyres – the usual.

'We're not all connected.'

Pale enough to be a vegan and a funny shine on her skin, greasy. 'Once you become accustomed to the idea you begin to feel it, you begin to be able to work with the energy.'

'We're not all connected.'

'It chimes in with quantum physics very nicely, but of course the philosophy is very ancient.'

'We are not all connected. We are bags of skin. We are all separate bags of thinking skin.'

Her mouth gave a tiny jerk. 'I'll just leave the leaflet.'

'You give me a way to stop thinking – I'll paper the whole bloody place with your leaflets. How about that. I'll give you the shop.'

She didn't look at him and didn't set down her leaflet.

'I meant it. You just let me know.' Shouting this at her back as she scurried to the door, escaped.

'You let me know.'

Then he sat at the till and rubbed his forehead.

He did that for a long while.

He wanted to go to Edinburgh.

SATURDAY TEATIME

So.

My head will keep on racing throughout this, I have no doubt.

Racing and running away.

Louping.

Breenjing.

Going a game with itself.

Which may well be a sign of weakness. Before I turned up I did need to consider my weaknesses and strengths, how best they'd be accommodated. In here I will have to be able to second-guess myself, but that won't be a problem – I've been doing it for years, because it is the key to any comfort.

Given that I want a happy time.

This is the general rule – people seek their happiness. Even if they're masochistic, when they find their perfect pain, it should make them happy.

And who doesn't like being happy? Happy's why I'm here. I am trying something new that should increase my happiness. This time it's *flotation and relaxation*. I've walked in and bought an hour of both.

At least, I suppose the *flotation* part is the one that's guaranteed and whatever *relaxation* I get will be down to me.

Quite possibly less than an hour of that.

And thereafter I'd expect an amount of happiness will ensue.

Anyway, I am predicting this is something I'll enjoy: floating, relaxing, unwinding, enjoying the benefits of salted water.

Whatever they are.

I'm not quite clear.

It feels slippery, somehow, the surface – slippery and thick. Not truly unpleasant and not exactly nice. Mainly neutral.

I did foresee the absence of distraction will leave me alone with me, which isn't always wise, but I've done what seemed necessary, sensible – I didn't bolt and clamber into this at once, there was no rush. I waited, pulled the door wide to let in the light and checked very thoroughly everywhere: each shadow, every corner, not forgetting above.

I am all that's here.

Leastways, there is me and there is here – which is a *Flotation Tank* – and, to be perfectly accurate, this isn't really a tank. Not anything like one.

I'd expected a tank.

Flotation Tank.

As advertised.

This is more of a room, a cupboard, in fact – a Flotation Damp Cupboard with Light-proof Door. A cupboard right down in the basement, as if they suffer persistent floods and have taken advantage.

No attempt at something futuristic, not a capsule and not a fancy casket affair, heavy lid on a watery grave.

Claustrophobia probably an issue with those options.

I'm just lying in some brine in a warm, wet cupboard. Who'd have thought.

But a warm, wet, *safe* cupboard – I've made myself entirely sure of that – just me and the four peaceful walls and the innocent ceiling, some water. Not even too much of that. Inches. Barely shin-deep.

And that's good, because now the door's shut it's as

dark as nasty thinking and I'd rather not end up imagining any possible cause for alarm. I'm naked and lying
with something I don't know – with the dark – and this
must seem only snug and homely, buoyant: no overtones
of drowning, suggestions of creatures that rise from
unlikely depths, hints of noise underneath the silence,
eager.

Which is more than enough of that.

Plus, it's thirty quid a session – stupid to waste it.
Embarrassing as well: running upstairs to the hippy at
the till after eight or nine minutes and saying you've had
to chuck it because of the monsters you brought in with
you, as if you're a kid.

Well, I can be definitive when I state there are no
monsters.

Not here.

I checked.

There's only myself in a peaceful setting, peaceful
cupboard, with an hour to reflect on the knowledge that
I must have more money than sense.

More money than sense – there are so many meaningless sayings we pass between ourselves.

Don't trust him as far as you can throw him.

There are always two sides to the argument.

He's not slow in coming forward.

She's no better than she should be.

This is the way to the flotation tank.

Sometimes, when you hear people talk, you'd imagine
that we are in some way obliged to take part in each
other's dreams, just plunge into lie after lie and wallow
about. You could think that on the inside we are mainly
fantasy.

Word dreams.

No internal organs, just a mass of unlikely excuses for
their absence.

And no way to stop the words.

No, there is, though.

There is.

I am in charge here.

That's right.

And nodding my agreement rocks the heart of everything.

Which is myself. For an hour.

They said doing this would make my head race.

A side effect of the floating.

Sensory deficit: not enough left of feeling to slow me down. Sleepy heart rate, skin quiet, almost disappeared, reality loosened and tepid, at body heat. I'm increasingly unclear about my edges, may have misplaced, or forgotten where I stop. I could, in fact, be seeping out into the water, could be washing away.

Best to take an inventory of what I am not.

Blinded heat. Scent of wet wood. Oddly substantial presence beneath the limbs – it now feels like a sofa, a mattress, a nothing that lets you hover, tip, spin. Gliding through your own little piece of outer space. No stars, though. Blanket blackness. Numb.

Not that I'm actually moving. At least I don't think so, I can no longer tell.

Need to be cautious about that.

Oh, and now I'm remembering that kid at the party last week.

Why not? I can let that happen.

He was scared of me at the start – I was, after all, an unknown visitor – but then we chatted and made faces and then he wasn't worried any more, was forgetting himself, giggling. He brought his hamster down to show me – Benny, Benji, Billy, doesn't matter.

He wants to go up your shirt.

Precocious idea. I mean, not sexual, but experimental. And I wasn't going to fight the child off – because that's how the hamster gets murdered and then there's hell to

60

pay – and the rest of the room was both crushingly middle-aged and viciously tedious so I'd no prospects of anything better to do and under the shirt goes the hamster.

The boy's seven, six, has purely innocent motivations, a generous impulse, and he sets the thing down on my stomach, gives me a sensation that he has already relished – the tiny paws and whiskers, scampers of fur across skin.

Lovely.

Weird and lovely.

That frantic ticking of breath – I'd known it before, years ago, and here it was back again: repeating, rattling along above its echo – because of course, I had a hamster when I was his age and of course I'd fed it into my own sleeves, my jumpers. It was something like sliding a panic inside my clothes: that scrabbling and vulnerability. I couldn't have said if I was reading its fear, or it was reading mine. The whole procedure was an adult kind of pleasure, complicated: anxiety and fun and loss of control and maybe the chance that I'd hurt it without meaning, or that it would hurt me.

I remember watching the boy's face and thinking that I ought to forget more, clean things out.

And then I picked up his hamster, held it firmly in my hand – that whole body reckless with life, the wild and tiny heart, everything about it too fragile.

The boy's eyes were happy and then less so.

I could feel his will between me and shutting my fist, the way he might be brave.

He looked, a loud look, and he was right to. He was a small, good-hearted man.

And then I gave the hamster back.

No harm done.

Not anywhere.

And none intended, not a breath.

But, let's be frank, a lousy choice of pet. Hamsters are almost impossible to love. They have the brains of a wind-up toy, or possibly a potato. They are bonsai rats and smell much worse than all that should imply. They're unconscious when you want to play with them, then berserk through every night, and they live for about a week. Flush the body down the toilet and buy another, I presume – it's not as if they cost a lot.

The kid's father was the sort who'd find that appealing. I was stuck in a corner with him for some truly geological slab of time while he maundered on about this probably mythical trip he made to Italy when he was younger and single and he took great pains to pronounce each Italian word as if he were a waiter in a sitcom and he leaned in tight and kept constructing these laborious smiles which I think were designed to imply that he was a dandy youngster and blade about town and could be that way again with no more than a cheap motel room and a free afternoon to spur him on.

He'd be the cheap motel breed of adulterer. Not for interesting and perverse reasons – just to save cash.

Fair enough, his wife is a dead-eyed, organic hummus-producing marionette with a whispery, creepy laugh – but he'll have made her that way. And she'll have made him a sticky-handed fraud reliant on alcohol, golf and non-threatening porn. They are every excuse they could ever need to abscond and yet they'll stay and, having ruined themselves and each other, they will grind on and on and their son will be worn down and hollowed at seventeen – a self-harmer, criminal, crackhead.

Hope not.

I'd like to think he'll muddle through.

Honest.

I wish him well.

And I was nice to him that evening.

Thank you very much. What a lovely hamster. Best I've seen. Is it time for you and him to go to bed? Oh, no, you're quite right. You go to bed, but he wakes up. That's how it works.

Night-night, anyway. Sleep tight. Well done, Barney, Buster, Bobby.

He told me the hamster's name and not his own.

Well done, you.

Once he'd gone I was by myself.

The solitary solitary, there on the lookout for fun.

More likely to find a sea lion in the hummus.

So by myself and bored.

But it's either that or I turn up on the doorstep with someone who isn't a date and then we spend our time explaining to couple after couple that we're just in the same room at the same time – no special bond, no special anything – just pals – to be frank, we're not even that – acquaintances – two people at loose ends simultaneously – although there was that kind of tension between us for a while – some years ago. And then it occurs to me, realisation seeping in, this might be the start of its resurrection – that particular discomfort might be resurrected – and I'm anxious because I don't want it, but will also be disappointed when he doesn't try anything. I will begin to feel ugly, unsuccessful. Meanwhile, all those inquisitions and explanations have become a burden and it's full night outside and I have decided I hate the man I came with. I will never see him again. He is a bastard. I won't even share a cab home with him because we are practically strangers and I don't really live in the same part of town and why should I, if I don't want to – I am a free agent and can control what I do.

At least, those parts of my life which are my own – those I can control. Those parts concerning other people, they are more problematic.

For example, I would rather not have been the solitary at that party.

If I'd had my own person there, someone I could have talked to, then we'd have hidden ourselves from the bowls of horrific salad and the nasty flans and we'd have chatted, maybe mentioned the hamster.

Yes, we'd have discussed the sensuality of hamsters and those rumours you always hear about film stars and gerbils. I don't see how that would be entertaining, trying to put a rodent in your anus, and surely the animal wouldn't cooperate. Or would you have it anaesthetised? Hypnotised? Trained? And you'd need a delivery system, some variety of piston, or at least a lubricated pipe. By the time you'd overcome the many challenges of insertion, would you still be aroused? Or are there people you can call who'll perform gerbil installations – professional and quick?

Thank you for phoning. Saturday night is a busy time for us, but please do leave your number and we'll reach you as soon as we can.

Candles and music. By yourself, or with a loved one, and this man there in overalls, smoking a Woodbine for effect and fitting your gerbil. Shaking his head and removing his flat cap when he doesn't quite like what he sees.

You've had some right cowboys in here . . . Any chance of a cuppa once I'm done?

We'd have talked, my companion and I, about that – about the way people find curious joys, will let themselves be borne along in hopes of them.

My joys would not encompass an evening hemmed in by magnolia woodchip and the reek of discontent while watching a mouth that I haven't the energy to loathe as it puckers and slackens and moistens and grins and no doubt tells me unseductive things about *Fi-ren-ze* and *Tor-in-o* and I have to picture plague rats cantering round inside snow globes up his arse so that I don't hit him.

That's what happens when I've no one to talk to.

I get annoyed.

Which is not relaxing.

But this is relaxing.

Should be relaxing.

I am here to relax.

Thread my hands in under the water and fold them smooth at the back of my neck, interlace the fingers. And this is like resting, if not relaxing. There's a flutter of instability as I reposition, the surface takes a while to settle, but I don't seem – for example – to be falling or anything like that, there's no unease, only a liquid shift against my spine that might be air, or time, intention, happiness.

The idea of falling, it's the only one I really wouldn't want to summon up.

The drop.

My theory about the drop.

We're born into it, slithering over its edges and into life and at the start it's exhilarating, it's a rush. We're flying. Almost. We're flying *down*. But we assume that if we were built to fly, if that's what we're for, then that's what we'll do. Forever. We imagine we'll plummet endlessly, perhaps in a broad, unnoticeable loop, a corkscrewing motion through infinity. We are not sure, we give it less than our full attention, because other bodies divert us, the ones who are falling at our pace. Our course screams onwards, downwards, and there they are, at our sides, near our faces, with us until the currents change, or else there's a torsion of breezes, or other processes we cannot quite explain, and they are gone and we are left to our descent.

It takes a while to realise every one of us will land and not survive it. We are a tragedy waiting to happen, or a design flaw, at the very least. And that murmur in our ears before we sleep – we imagined it was blood flow, heartbeats, tinnitus – but it's not, it's the drop. It's whatever's left lashing past you, piece by piece, soaring up out of reach: minutes pulled to rags, ripped out of hours, days, weeks – it's falling.

But let's not get dragged off into that.

Not here.

Not now.

Floating is what we're here for now – not falling – today we are being sustained.

All's well.

I couldn't have a theory about puppies, rainbows, laughter. It has to be a meditation on the meaningless brevity of existence.

No days off with me.

Myself and I.

And then there's the other theory – the one about laughter.

No. Leave that one be.

But I do have a theory about laughter.

Which isn't what I want to think of here.

Shouldn't let it seep out and colour the water, taint it, change its grip.

And, then again, I can't avoid it now.

So.

Laughter. That unmistakable sign of happiness. The first time you hear it for real, kicking out of your head, that punch of sound – then you know everything at once. You've got the truth of it right there, wet against your tongue.

The warm noise curled against your tongue.

Like here.

Like now.

Adrift in the truth of something – the taint of that.

No, my mouth is empty as my mind.

No, not so.

I was older than the kid at the party when I found out about laughter. Saturday teatime in the family house, that tall and narrow house, and I'm nine. I seem to remember myself being nine, and with my friend – acquaintance, anyway. I make my pals one at a time and without enthusiasm, pick vaguely sadistic loners with an intensity about them. This isn't a pattern I wish to repeat, but occasionally I can't help it.

And I'm watching television, sitting on the floor and too close to the screen – one or other of my parents would have views about that, would express them, but they're busy. My pal is behind me and she is uncomfortable and I don't care. As of this afternoon, I hate her. By next week we will never speak again.

And I am laughing.

I am laughing more loudly than I ever have. I believe I am laughing more loudly than I ever will.

My acquaintance is not laughing.

This makes sense because we are not watching a funny programme, we are watching *Doctor Who*, which is science fiction, children's science fiction – running about and monsters and saving the day – and the Doctor has pals and saves them, too, or they save him, or even when he dies, he doesn't quite leave them, he bounces right back looking like a different actor and everything goes on just as it was – running about and monsters and saving the day. It's very exciting but slightly frightening as well and so it doesn't often make me laugh.

But I'm laughing today. I can't stop.

When I was younger my parents would wonder aloud if the show wasn't overly worrying for me – things that were threatening walking up out of the sea, minds being taken over and running away, louping, breenjing, scared soldiers firing bullets that never worked, never prevented the bad things on the way. I wanted to watch, though. I wanted that small way of being terrified.

I am watching now and unconcerned by what I see and from upstairs, coming in through the ceiling, there are noises – not completely familiar, but I understand

67

them. I have heard things like them before. And I am still laughing, howling, hurting my throat, and then I stand and swallow and I say, 'Excuse me,' to my acquaintance and I walk from the room and then run, take the stairs two at a time and across the landing and there is the door to my parents' bedroom and it is locked.

I didn't know that it could lock.

This brings about a complicated adult feeling, because inside the room is my mother – I can hear her squealing sometimes, these cries – and my father is with her, hitting her again – this time he is hitting her so much that there are other sounds of impacts against the walls, or the floor, of furniture shifting, clatters – and I cannot get in to stop this, but I know that I couldn't anyway – not even if the door were open, pulled wide, and the light running up into every corner.

I don't want to see what's in there. I am glad that I'm locked out. This makes me a bad child, a bad daughter.

I hammer on the door while knowing my acquaintance will hear this along with all the rest which my laughing couldn't cover but at least I tried. And I don't want to be let in. I am lying with the whole of myself, pretending I've come to save her, stop him, when inside I know that I can't because I'm too frightened.

But maybe my hammering will make things better, change them.

But that's another lie. I know the way my parents are – if I hammer but I can't get in then they won't notice and nothing will be different, only more of the same. I am embarrassed for being a bad child and ashamed for turning into this lie and for going downstairs again to see my acquaintance and say, 'Sorry about that,' in exactly the way my father and my mother tell their acquaintances, 'Sorry about that,' when something unimportant has gone wrong.

I sit down and start laughing again.

I look at the screen.

And here's the Doctor with the hat and the curly hair and the great big eyes. I've always liked him. The episode when he arrived to replace the preceding Doctor, I remember being nervous and little and troubled by change. I was trying to guess if he'd be nice and all right – keeping cautious the way that I might when I get a new teacher – and it took such a lovely short time to know he could be relied upon, was fine. The Doctor does what he ought to, sorts things out. He opens doors when they need to be opened and he locks them when they should be shut and he shouts at important people who don't expect it and he makes them listen and be sensible. I'm no longer young enough to believe that he exists, but he's a good idea, entirely good, and when I'm by myself I still like to concentrate hard on the pictures that start each episode, because they haze forward and forward, seem like a tunnel to something, I don't know what, but I'm quite sure I wouldn't mind it. I would go there. I'd be brave. I have heard people talk about meditation and hypnosis and I imagine this is mine.

My acquaintance usually doesn't enjoy the show, doesn't want to talk about it on Monday mornings, has no interest in how the adventure is getting along. This is another reason to dislike her. She is also why my parents are upstairs – my father knew he could get away with this while I had company and would be trapped into being polite. I have been brought up nicely, to entertain visitors, to be caught.

And I am still laughing.

This keeps on without any effort from me and is part of the sounds of the house and not mine.

I am also staring at the screen, but can't follow the story – that's an irritation – like the way they move the programme around, so you have to check when it starts – fifteen minutes later, five earlier, you never know – and maybe the cooking smells are nagging through at me, because it's almost time for tea, but I can't go yet because it hasn't finished and I have to be near the adventures and soak up their happiness, their braveness, so I can take it in with me to the table where she'll be defenceless, so soft that it makes me angry, and he'll be complaining about the food, or asking me questions I can't quite answer. He'll be starting to build a fight and she will be in a kind of free fall and I won't feel like eating, but if I can't then that will be a problem and one more reason for an argument, because if there is something wrong with me then he will hurt her, so there can never be a single thing that's wrong with me.

I am old enough to see that I can't stand this – can't stand him as he is, or her as she is – I cannot stand this any more. But I do have to. This is clear.

It is also clear that I want to be able to shout at them, to explain, 'There is nothing that fucking frightens me more than you, there never fucking was and never fucking will be. It's you I shouldn't have to fucking watch. And I don't want to be either of you and I know I will be both.'

Because I am old enough to fucking swear.

And I'd maybe end up laughing afterwards, I can't guess and won't find out, because I'll never shout a word at anyone – too polite.

Laughing now, though.

Before I run up to my own room – forget I should excuse myself to my acquaintance, I just leave her and go to find my little hatchet. I've started collecting hard-edged tools, pseudo-weapons. It's not as if I'll ever use them, but I do like to have them around, and I run more, out on the landing, stop at my parents' door and clatter the hatchet against it. I barely dent the wood and I am worried I will get in trouble and worried that my mother's dying, will be dead, and worried that my hatchet might hurt someone in my family.

70

I have a family.

There are three of us.

I hate the three of us but not enough, not yet.

Because this part of me is still waiting for everything to turn out well.

I still expect myself to save the day.

But all I do is laugh.

Which is making the sound of hurt things, who are trying not to be, falling things who are trying not to be, dying things who are trying to bounce back, looking like a different actor so that everything goes on just as before.

Which is my theory about laughter.

For what it's worth.

Which puts the poison in the water, the bad colour in the slippery dark.

You have to go and spoil things. Every time.

So change the subject.

Be elsewhere.

He mainly had dusty shoes, that Doctor – scuffed about and covered in pale dust, as if he'd been surviving, travelling all his life, as far away as he could be. I loved it when he wore the dusty shoes.

But I ought to forget more, clean things out.

Headache at the thought of so much memory, of me.

And I think that I'm crying – the water jolting in around me, the torn breath – I definitely think I may be crying – salt to salt.

I know what I'm like.

This need to be happy, to be solitary, to have someone of my own, to be brave, loved, hated, terrified, to make a family, to stay without one, to find the perfect pain.

I know.

This mess.

This awful mess.

I know.

To be rid of it, bounce back and start again.
With dusty shoes.
They would be the best thing and the safest.
Forget that I ever expected to save the day and never try again and put on my shoes and get running, get racing away.
This is all I want now – dusty shoes.
I'd be happy with that.

CONFECTIONER'S GOLD

They are both almost used to this, their tiredness. Two days now without sleeping, not even a nap since they got here.

Which was on Friday – when they got here.

It was definitely Friday and they have kept very firm about this, because in retrospect their movements are unlikely, unclear. For example, after the Friday they ran clean on through a Saturday that seemed to exist for only an hour or two – the length of a rain shower and a squabble, a slammed door – and then it became the unfamiliar Sunday which currently surrounds them, insistent and over-bright. This is obstinately Sunday and lunchtime and the pavement is unsteady as they walk. It dodges playfully underneath their feet and either shakes the man towards the woman, or else shakes them apart. They cannot decide which is more unbearable.

The man swallows and feels his throat raw after so much talking, shouting, talking. His face, eyes, scalp, plus the whole of the area where he used to think – he is sure that he used to be able to think – the whole of his head feels only weak and blunted and slightly dry. He can't tell if he's still blinking, but isn't sure if he'd be able to go without. Against the inside of his forehead, he can feel her voice – Elaine's voice – repeating his name – *Tom* – it scuffs at the bone – *Tom* – and is apparently not just his name any more, but also an accusation.

Tom is as certain as he can manage that he wants to

sleep very soon and then wake up not Tom at all, not responsible, at the very least, not here. He would like to be surrendered, to admit defeat.

While Tom wonders if they ought to stop for coffee and if even that might be impossible, Elaine is at the edge of enjoying how difficult it has become to lift one foot and set it forward, hoist the other, then the same again. She finds the process fascinating.

This is strolling.

This is us strolling.

It also occurs to her that they ought to be hand in hand, herself and her man.

Two lovers strolling together.

Two relatively young people who have sex with each other strolling together.

Two very close to middle-aged people who are scared of having sex with each other strolling together.

Two people strolling.

If you over-think things, then they get away from you.

Anyway, she's almost convinced they should be reaching out for what they know, holding on while the day swims and finding comfort in themselves. But they can't do that. Not at the moment. They are no use.

She hunches her fingers in against each other – as if she might be able to hold an idea and be satisfied with that. Then she realises this will look as if she's clenching her fists – because she *is* clenching her fists – and she gives up, opens her palms to the cold again. She has no gloves because she's lost them, dropped them, set them down in a stupid place and gone away. Another mistake.

Tom is remembering the Blind School at the corner of their street, which is a completely unhelpful thing to do. The Blind School depresses him. And since he's already depressed, the Blind School will depress him more, so he should ignore it, avoid it, but he can't.

76

He's too weary for that kind of fight – for every kind
of fight.

*They're pathetic – the blind. But not the way they should
be pathetic.*

No, they shouldn't *be pathetic.*

That's the problem.

Probably.

They are pathetic and they shouldn't be.

*Hands waving, sticks waving, they're totally out of control –
they make the whole street look post-apocalyptic. It's hopeless.
I end up feeling sorry for them and I'm not supposed to, I'm
supposed to feel* empathy, *not* sympathy *– here I am, a human
being and they're human beings, too – only with this extra
thing, this visual impairment thing, but they're also human
beings and that's how we keep our mutual respect, by knowing
that we're the same species, no matter what. That's your dignity,
right there, that is.*

*Except anyone who's like me would have no dignity, that
would be gone.*

*And if the blind are pathetic and lost – like they've been
let outside randomly – recklessly – each of them needing help,
a lot of help, total assistance, asking strangers to lead them,
guide them, haul them over roads – then what does that imply?
If we're linked, then what does that say about me? Or if they
end up standing, blank and standing, like people who have no
idea of what's in their own pockets – then I do not wish to
empathise.*

*Or are the blind testing us: the sighted: me? Are they checking
we'll pitch in and be Samaritans? Would they be that perverse?*

*Not that the blind shouldn't be perverse. They should have
the right.*

*Unless it's the school that's playing games: some twisted kind
of institution. What does it teach them? Exactly? Anything?
Basket-weaving? Mattress-making? Piano-tuning? Traditional
blind stuff? Forensic anthropology? I mean, they should learn all
the things that anyone could know, not just the blind stuff: being*

a switchboard operator, that stuff. I think they used to have blind switchboard operators. Of course they should learn everything, absolutely should – but crossing roads, too – not being killed, not getting hurt in preventable tragedies, that's what I'd say.

They can't see, so they need to be trained in improvisation.

Human beings, they need to be safe: no tragedy, no oncoming car, just you with your own name and no worries, happy.

Every time he steps beyond what is currently his front door, he feels angry on the blind people's behalf and also tries not to identify with them, not to find them grotesquely bewildered in a way that reflects quite badly on his life. And when he comes home – when he's tired and perhaps apprehensive, given what's going on with Elaine and with all of the crap that is worse than Elaine – then the blind become a pantomime of every bloody sadness in the world. And he is a sadness, too, it can't be denied, along with everything he touches. And his heart cramps as his key slips in the lock.

It's pure self-obsession – disgusting – I only care about the blind, because they're me.

I have decided they are me. All of them, a crowd of me.

Truth is, the only people who ever get my full attention have to be exactly like me, have to be me, as if they're pieces of my head.

She's right.

Elaine's right.

She isn't me and she is right.

That's when I'm interested.

Otherwise I'm mainly not.

I'd have to be this tired to admit it, because I like to be good, to believe that I am decent, but I'm not.

But she's a bitch to say it.

Lately, he has been trying, as a discipline, to maintain a positive mental state. But when he's being negative about something which is, itself, negative, does that doubled negative count as a positive?

*And none of the blind are Caucasian, why is that? The
school is only for the non-white blind? They segregate the blind,
first and second class, according to race? Is that why it's useless?
A second-class type of school?*

Who would think like that?

Would I think like that?

*When I take their arms, do the leading, get them over the
road, I don't like to talk to them, not really, does that mean
I'm racist? If they were white, would I tell them when they're
covered in crumbs they can't see, would I point out their different
types of disarray?*

Or do I say nothing because they're blind?

Am I prejudiced in that way, too?

Am I a bastard?

I think I am.

Quite possibly.

A total bastard.

And my wife would agree.

Is that a positive – because we agree?

Tom needs a coffee, but suspects he can't drink any
more – not without actually having a heart attack. Still,
he would enjoy the smell of it and folding his hands
outside the mug, that warmth. Before he's checked if his
tone will sound all right, he discovers that he's already
asked Elaine, 'Would you like a coffee?'

'I don't know. You would?' Her tone isn't all right.

'Don't do that.' Nor is his. Again.

'What?'

'Then, if I say yes, it's like I'm making you have a
coffee and everything has to be about what I want and
if I say no, it's like I'm not letting you have one when
you do want one – you just . . . I want to sit down
somewhere warm.'

'Okay.' Elaine intended to say something else – something like *no* – or, *stop reading things into every bloody word
I say, Jesus, if I started reading things into you, I'd be busy,*

79

I'd have a full-time job on my hands, I'd have to take evening classes – instead of evening work to make up for the job you don't have any more – but even preparing the shapes of that for her tongue feels exhausting and she is, in any case, worn back to the sense that she is hungry and cold, that she also needs to sit down somewhere warm. 'We could have lunch. Tom? We could do that.' She is simple, just very simple inside herself.

Tom's eyes are pinkish, distressed. She isn't sure how long they've been this way. He hasn't cried, not today – not as far as she knows – but he does look awful, wrung out, and she is a bad person for making no effort to support him. Bad wife. And he is a bad husband for forcing her to conclude that she's a bad wife.

He's not a bad man, though. It wasn't his fault he lost the job – not his mistake. That's half the trouble, they barely did make a mistake: only these little tiny wrong judgements: but they're ruined all the same. They might as well have been careless.

'Yes. Yeah. Why not.' His voice is flattened now, blanked.

Which should make her sympathetic, only today she resents him for hiding what he feels. She hates it when he's secretive.

They both swing slightly too quickly in towards the next restaurant they see, which is Japanese – they aren't all that fond of Japanese – and which they know will be expensive. The whole avenue up this high is expensive – glistening shops and men in overworked shoes and dandy overcoats, women with immobile hair, immobile faces, aggressive jewellery. Tom and Elaine find themselves surrounded by an atmosphere of fussy cleanliness, of demands pending and important expectations that should be met. This, in addition to their own atmosphere – the one which is more like a migraine, or a bereavement – the one which means they are about to spend more money they can't afford, because the new worry this will give them – such a manageably small cause for concern – this will be a distraction, almost a type of joke.

Tom opens the restaurant door. Rubbing up against the hot curve of his skull comes – *this is Elaine, a person you used to like.*

Out of habit, he lets her go before him and start to climb the narrow stairs.

Time was, you'd have enjoyed this. You'd have wanted to watch her arse. This is Elaine's arse, an arse you used to like. Worse than that – you still like it.

So, Elaine first and then Tom, they bump upwards on the suddenly draining flight of steps. It seems tactless that when they emerge at the top they have to stand side by side and hear the catch and fall of breath in each other's throats, their mouths. The air up here is snug and peaceful and is scented gently, perhaps by seaweed, certainly by something salt. They wait, stare at the mostly empty tables. They sway – or the room does – either way, it's something they can't help.

Elaine's elbow nudges Tom and flinches back, denies the contact. She is reversing their process, unpicking how they used to be. When she began to love him, her body knew it first and as soon as they were over, it knew that, too. Time was, it would set her hand at the small of his back, would lean in for him when they walked, brush his shoulder, and she would go home once they'd parted and realise how clearly she remembered every touch, although each had been involuntary. She would watch herself taking things for him, holding on. She'd kept his jacket while he'd looked for his keys on that night they'd parked outside his house and simply stayed there, never gone in, and then she'd set the jacket down and kept him instead and they'd lost hours in the car, burned up hours, not looking for anything except themselves, the good parts of themselves hidden in each other.

But once you start that, you find all kinds of rubbish. In the end you can't work out who disgusts you more.

A waitress appears neatly from behind a curtain and leads them to a table which is not by the window, although Tom notices there are three tables which *are* by the window and only one of them is occupied. He feels he might remonstrate with the woman, complain. Then again, he and Elaine are perhaps so obviously unhappy that they'll be seated away from others, no matter where they go, in case they cause a scene, or simply demoralise couples with less experience.

And maybe I only want to complain because she's Japanese. Maybe I hate Japanese human beings, too.

The couple who are sitting by the window, they're Japanese. Maybe the waitress hates white human beings and they never get to sit where it's light.

I would like that – to be hated by someone who doesn't know me, loathed for no reason.

The waitress smiles at him. 'Would you prefer to sit in the window?'

'No. No.' This is the wrong thing to say, because Elaine may prefer this and he should ask her. 'At least . . . Elaine?'

'I don't care where we sit.' She has taken off her coat and is comfortable and wishes to Christ that Tom didn't make an opera out of everything. 'And might I have some green tea? Would you like tea, Tom?' The sound of *tea, Tom* almost makes her laugh. These days she is often close to laughing. 'Tea, Tom?' It sounds like a cracked little bell, or a cracked little life: the way they'd intended to be. It is funny – as funny as falling in love, or having plans.

'Tea? Oh. Yes. Thanks.'

Elaine watches Tom frown at the retreating waitress. He never does know how to deal with service providers – checkout assistants, bag-packers, waitresses, the doorman in their borrowed flat – they make him blush. She used to wait on tables when she was a student and therefore knows it's best to be a firmly courteous and straightforward customer. And you ought to tip well.

We shouldn't tip at all. Shouldn't be here. Borrowing Paul's flat – Madison Avenue and someone on duty twenty-four hours a day to help you work the lift, press the button for you, in case you don't want to, or you're tired. Bet they've never seen tired like us.

Shit.

We're idiots.

Should have stayed in Chicago.

Should have stayed in Edgbaston and never even tried to come over here.

At least when you fuck up at home you're still at home.

Their tea arrives in a heavy, red-glazed pot they both find well made, pleasing – and they say so carefully, also complimenting the tiny, matching cups – and each of them picks the same bento box from the menu because then they get a little of most things and won't be jealous of each other's choices.

They are polite.

'The miso soup was good.'

'It said they make their own tofu.'

'I wonder what that involves.'

'I have no idea.'

Tom saying this last so apologetically that Elaine does let herself smile, in the hope that smiling will be like releasing a laugh in stages. 'I don't know, either.'

'The little cube of beef – is it that kind they get from those cows they massage and feed beer to, or sake? The special cows? It's – whatever it is – it's . . . lovely.'

Tom guesses this will be the best Japanese food he'll ever taste: miniature portions of nameless fish, perfect slices of strange vegetables, great rice. He feels most secure about judging the rice, since they eat it so frequently now – filling and cheap, like chips.

Grew up on chips. So many years and I'm that much further forward – from chips to rice. Not Freedom Fries, not French Fries, not Fries – chips. Salt and fat and bulk and starch to imitate contentment, fill you up.

This meal he finds ludicrously moving, perhaps enraging, too. It's set out like a series of gifts, special delicacies nestling in lacquered boxes, as if someone back behind that curtain is fond of them, wants them to thrive.

Their usual customers here, he is sure, demand these levels of faked affection as a matter of course and that is offensive, but still this strange kind of love is also disarming, intoxicating. 'You know . . .' He does, in fact, think that he will cry soon because of it. 'I'm worth two hundred and fifty thousand dollars. I found out.' This is not what Tom anticipated saying.

'What?' Elaine has spent the last six months signing cheques with an unverifiable version of her signature, so that enquiries will be made and toing and froing will ensue, this causing delays in the removal of money from their account – money which is not their money, but an idea of money, an idea they pay for, more and more. Tom is staring at her. His expression has a sort of yowl in it, something intent. She prepares to say, 'What are you talking about – you're not worth anything.' And realises how that will sound, even if she adds, 'I'm not worth anything, either.' By then it would be too late, damage done.

'I'm worth two hundred and fifty thousand dollars.'

Something in the light around her sparks for a moment and then contracts, because whatever he means won't be real, can't be real. 'Tom, please. Don't.'

'I read an article. It's if you sold me. Corneas, bone grafts, tendons – that way, I'm worth two hundred and fifty thousand dollars. Skin – they even sell your skin. To people who need skin. Burned people. You have a legacy. You make the blind see.' This, he completely should not have said – it leaves him swallowing, clamping his jaw and the tears seeping out, becoming obvious, and his nose is running and he realises he is worried that the waitress will find him pathetic, not empathetic. He can't predict what Elaine will find him.

'I'm eating. You're talking about somebody selling your skin while I'm eating.'

Elaine knows she ought to be angry – that would be completely justified – him dropping over into self-pity the way that he does and trying to haul her down, too – but it's such a strong, unnerving thought – her husband dead and therefore blameless – which she hadn't expected, but that's how he seems, this imagined corpse – and no one to defend him: not her, not anyone – so he is not only dead and blameless, but lonely and unloved and open to let someone creep in and steal what he was. 'Tom.' If she moves, lets her fingers settle on his free hand, or holds his arm – if she feels him shivering – and it is clear that he is shivering and all the cold of the world is in him and the cold of how they are and have to be – if she does that, touches him, there is no telling what will happen. Her husband scares her.

Tom is aware that he is both weeping and shaking and that he's doing so mostly because of the meal. The other sadnesses are too enormous and he can't currently consider them, but he has to admit he is spoiling this marvellous food by loving it to the point where it wracks his heart and this is insane and also means that he's a whole new kind of wasteful bastard.

'Come on, love. Tom.'

Her voice is kind. It'll be that way out of habit, he supposes.

'Tom.' Elaine supposes he enjoys being ill. 'You'll make yourself poorly.' She's noticed before that he can sicken, get real symptoms, vomiting, aches, when he doesn't want to do something, meet someone.

It may not be deliberate. He could be improperly balanced, prone to psychosomatic trauma. Unsuitable for sale, in fact. 'Tom. Please get a grip.' He could be unfairly in need of protection. 'Look, the waitress is coming. Please. For me. Please, sweetheart.'

And the waitress does come and pauses by their table while Tom looks up at her, blurry, and Elaine presents what she knows will be nothing like a smile.

'Is everything . . .'

Elaine watches as the woman falters. It's plain to all three of them that any enquiry about their meal is going to prove indelicate.

Is everything all right? – No, it's not.

Can I get you anything? – What do you suggest? Do you have a gun, or a pair of matching nooses, or two hundred and fifty thousand dollars – so that my husband won't have to sell himself as meat – just two hundred and forget the fifty, what's fifty thousand dollars between friends?

'Are you . . .' The waitress steadies and adjusts, 'Happy with your meal?'

'Yes.' Elaine nods to underline this. The laugh has spun in at her, is winding, drilling, it is making her spine seem fibrous, tinder dry. 'Yes. And some more, some more tea and we'll have a dessert.' Why not? This was costing them fifty dollars each already – fifty, fifty thousand, what's fifty? – they might as well get a dessert.

Tom feels he should be explanatory and adds, 'We lost . . .' and then can't begin to say what. Not that *We lost* doesn't pretty much cover it. The waitress nods softly and he believes that he likes her and she likes him and that he needs to grasp these moments, collect them.

Empathy.

Elaine dabs at the back of his hand for a moment and news of this travels slowly up his arm.

'Do you think you'll want a pudding?' She pats his knuckles. 'Tom? Might as well. I will if you will.' There's a flare of motion she doesn't expect and then her hand is caught between both of his, held in a hot, damp pressure. She faces him, blinks, 'Have to build you up – then you'll be worth more.'

And this sounds too likely and too close, so they keep their hands stacked on the table, a confinement they find reassuring.

Elaine even wonders about adding to it, completing the set: *hands, two pairs, any reasonable offer will be considered.*

Tom feels very slightly as if he has sprung across at her fleeing some unspecified peril and is now clinging.

For dear life.

He could let go. At any point. Just not this one.

We'll need to stay with her parents – bloody Edgbaston – it was bad enough living there by ourselves – arsehole bloody schoolkids hanging around – little pothead wankers and skinny, horsey tarts who throw up all the time. And their arsehole bloody parents.

And her arsehole bloody parents. You're from Cumbernauld? Oh, well.

Can't go and stay with the Ma, though. All settled in Brodick – sea views and Dad scattered on the beach. Worked himself hollow to buy me an education, the start of a life where this shite wouldn't happen. Oh, well. Can't even tell the Ma how things turned out. America? It all went tits up. Oh, well. Government bailed the banks out, but not us. Oh, well. First hired, first fired, crucifying fucking mortgage and not citizens. Oh fucking, fucking, well.

No swearing, though. And positive. We won't be homeless. We'll be in Edgbaston.

They let each other go when the waitress clears their table and returns with plates of minute rectangular desserts – two pink, two cream, two chocolate brown with a brush of gold leaf on the top.

'We should scrape it off and save it.' Although saying

so makes Tom feel hemmed in rather than jovial. 'Gold – the only stuff that's worth anything. Should have bought shares.'

Elaine slowly puts her fork into the pink, lifts up a beautiful fragment and eats. 'God, it's wonderful. Sort of a mousse, or something. Very strawberry.'

They both manage the pink and the cream and softly agree they were ridiculously, unnecessarily fine and then they stare at the chocolate and the flakes of gold.

'Confectioner's gold. Is there such a thing?' Elaine remembers she read somewhere that the secret way to win your man is by asking him questions and not knowing answers, deferring to the wisdom he wants you to prove he has. But Tom isn't like that.

'Well, if there is, we've got some.'

Elaine hears his voice getting thinner, stressed. Tom her man, Tom who's snuffling and wiping his face with the heel of his hand, who's too much a boy. She tells him, as if this might cheer him up, 'I bet people come in here all the time and just order it. Plate of gold, please.' Tom the boy who is a lecturer, letters after the name and a Dr in front – Tom who is still always waiting to be found out – she never has made him any more secure than that. 'Plate of gold. Like eating money.'

'Like eating something better than money.'

Tom clears his throat, readies his forefinger and thumb, flexes, picks up the soft chocolate between them and puts it all into his mouth, lets it warm, melt, cloy. He doesn't chew, only swallows and so tomorrow he'll be partly gold. He'll incorporate it, never let it go.

Or else this is just a waste. An intolerable waste.

There's something like fright in him, vertigo. He watches Elaine's face, something about her expression which is brave: small and courageous and enough to make him bleed, shout, touch her, although he does none of those things, only watches as she picks up the last of

88

their meal, repeats his gestures, studies the shape and then eats it, swallows gold.

Afterwards, they head for the park, the sun dropping fast through the afternoon, already striking fire in the highest windows of the mountainous apartment blocks. Elaine sees her husband tread across a tangle of long shadows, then lean against the tree that cast them. He appears to be almost relaxed. The size of him – almost clumsy, but he never is – and the line of his back: when it softens he can seem like he used to be, the last three years driven off, cured. Maybe this is the secret way to keep her man – never look at his face.

Almost clumsy.

Sometimes completely clumsy. I used to think I'd say something – that there are nights when he'd want to please me, but he already had. Anxious fingers. Insisting. Too much.

Big hands.

He has stupid, magnificent, big hands.

And he isn't clumsy any more. Isn't anything.

Maybe this is the secret way to keep each other – never look and never touch. Never meet.

They wander in among the leaves and American robins, the flicker of sparrows, and then they deliver themselves to increasingly wider paths until they are easing along beside the road, heading out to the dimming streets. The light is bitter and behind them a bright haze of red is rising to finish the day.

By the time they get back to their borrowed apartment they are both a dead cold, slurred with exhaustion. Tom considers running a bath and then decides against it. Elaine makes them someone else's excellent coffee in someone else's excellent mugs and they sit on someone else's excellent sofa and stare out at someone else's excellent rooftop view, the wild shapes the city hides up against the sky: bell towers, temples, pinnacles, farmhouse verandas, nunnery gardens, buttresses and battlements: the fantasies that money conjures and maintains. The sunset leaps and gilds a tower block downtown and off to their west, makes it burn so sharply that it leaves a numbness when they turn away and marks wherever they look.

In the morning, they have to leave here. They don't want to go.

WHOLE FAMILY WITH YOUNG CHILDREN DEVASTATED

This was yesterday.

No, this was earlier today. This was 2.56 in the morning and I was brutally awake and very much unable to remember asking anyone to phone up and make me listen to their house.

That's all I could hear, just their house – the sound of their furniture, perhaps, a room with ornaments and carpet, the kind of space that wouldn't raise a din: muffled, cosy, none of that messy background you'd get from a mobile, or a late-night place of work, this was the noise of a person waiting in their home, not moving and not speaking, not a word.

And I imagined this person standing, sneaking their breath out and maybe their free hand weighted at their side, hanging – or maybe both hands dropped and the receiver pointless, as if they can no longer think what they should do. They were already making me feel compassionate.

An aeroplane worried distantly off to the east. Far and high.

I had no memory of reaching for the phone, which meant that had happened while I was unconscious. I was already aware that, like many people, I can perform complex series of actions without myself. This is handy.

I believed that I hadn't spoken and positive that he hadn't, either – or she hadn't – the person. There was only this concentrating silence that tunnelled in along the line, dragging a sense of my possible counterpart and their receiver, the curl of their fingers, a suggestion of their sweat. Late-night calling always does suggest some kind of sweat, the symptoms of personal emergency, unpredictable elements: pain, fear, failure to halt appropriately, removal of comforts and dignity, sex.

Something in those areas.

That was my guess.

And by this time I should have hung up, or shouted *hello* with increasing alarm, the way people do in horror movies when the killer has cut their connection, when there will soon be a murderer in their house. Instead I smiled.

I don't believe that smiles are audible.

But as soon as I happened to make one, the line snapped shut.

I rolled over and dipped back into sleep, stretched out my arm to catch at it, grab the doze, the ringing doze.

Which wasn't sensible, wasn't possible – a ringing doze, that was a source of confusion.

The telephone ringing again.

And I needn't have answered.

But I had this idea now of the person standing, someone who might need something, might need me – and that sound in itself, the ring, is intentionally demanding and who was I to think I should resist? Plus there was a more than average chance the call might even be for me, the start of a proper conversation.

So.

'Hello.' I made a point of speaking loudly. I was abrupt in my manner.

'Ah . . . I'm sorry.' A man's voice, muffled with a kind of indecision, but no more dramatic emotions than that.

There's this other voice, too, shrill and hacking up behind his words. '*Go on. Tell her. Her.*' A woman is shouting, '*Go on! Try it – as if . . .*' She's at a slight distance, '*as if!*' although not so far away that she *has* to shout. '*Go on! You called her, you tell her, you just fucking tell her.*' She is plainly screaming because she wants to, because her emotions *are* dramatic and are leading her that way.

And the man – who may be stunned by his situation – murmurs in with, 'Ah, yes . . . I'm sorry. I didn't mean to –' and then he stops.

'*Bastard.*'

I have to assume he is pondering what he should say. Clearly he'd like to prove for the screaming woman that he doesn't know me, so he can't simply offer, 'I didn't mean to call you.' That implies former acquaintance. He may also wish to seem incapable of sustaining an interaction as sophisticated as an affair – and he *has* succeeded – as far as I can tell – in sounding quite stupid. If I were him I might reel off *sorry* for as long as I could, but then would that mean I was sorry for getting caught rather than sorry for inconveniencing a stranger? It would be hard to tell.

Half asleep, I can't think of suggestions which might be useful and, in any case, it's 3 a.m. and someone who knows this man – someone who sounds like a wife – is screaming at him in his house. No advice could save him at this point.

He starts again, 'I was the wrong number. When I rang a few minutes ago.'

'*Bastard. You think I believe –*'

There is the sound of some object dropping, perhaps breaking, in a way that is violent and yet unclear. '*Fu-cking. Bas-tard.*' The woman's voice sheers off on her final syllable and subsides.

The man is whispering by this time, 'I am very sorry. I didn't . . .' His voice seems to huddle in close.

And I am immediately very sorry, too. 'Yes. Yes, I know.' Even though I have been inconvenienced, I do want to show solidarity.

'Do you?'

There's an odd shade of innocence in his question which makes me need to reassure. I try, 'Well, I . . .' and run out of gentleness after two syllables.

'*Fucker!*'

Another object, undoubtedly glass, hits an unforgiving surface with audible results and I say, less kindly than I might have hoped, 'I'm going to hang up now. Goodnight.'

Of course, I shouldn't have said *goodnight* to him. I should have said *good morning*.

Ten minutes later, he made his third call. Or else, I supposed it might be the screaming woman this time, whoever she was: pressing redial, wanting to scream at *me* now and badger out a vindicating truth. So I raised the receiver and slapped it down again at once.

The phone rang repeatedly after that, but I ignored it, let it drill and drill, not giving up, until I had to disconnect it at the wall, listen to the milder nagging from the kitchen and the living room. In the end I unplugged the whole lot, silenced my home as an intruder might. Then I crept through and watched my television.

The twenty-four-hour news was reviewing some survey: an occupied population soon happier with lowered death tolls, but worried by abductions and also rapes. Mutilations up 15 per cent. Degrees of normality returning, expectations readjusted, many officials pleased. Pictures of sand and litter, a low house with something uneasy about it, out of kilter – I don't see it long enough to find out what, because I change the channel, because I don't need to be depressed.

Getting by, that's my aim, locating and holding on tight to whatever will bowl me along. I value fitness, sanity, a pattern of healthy and restful nights, survival. And when I can't rest, I watch the call-in shows. They help.

They also make it wonderfully clear that people throughout the country are wakeful as I am and ringing up strangers – television's friendly strangers – and they're paying to call and guess out mysterious things: what names might be included in a list of celebrity chefs, or prominent adulterers, or which fatal diseases can be spelled within a thirty-letter grid, or what could have been blanked out from famous headlines, popular proverbs, debt collector's letters, rules of engagement – the details don't matter, the sleepless are eager to take part. They'll try roulette, they'll chat about their relatives, they'll buy jewellery, adjustable ladders, craft supplies, they'll call psychics and spend warm, expensive minutes hearing the news from tarot cards, rune stones, star signs, the I Ching – they're happy to be game for anything. As long as there's somebody inside the screen talking back like a loud relation – or maybe not someone that close, more likely a visitor from a local church, or perhaps a nurse – as long as the sense of being cared for is filling up their room. I can understand that.

Last night I watched a woman with an honest face – dyed hair and a caring manner – she extrapolated karma and future events from birth dates and vocal auras. She talked quite slowly, comfortingly, didn't badger, 'Love and light to you, Leo girl, and what I'm getting here is that he's afraid. I know you haven't heard from him, not for six months, but that's because he's afraid. Men, we know men, they have to work out their feelings and sometimes it's difficult for them to confront, to deal with them, the way we have to. I do see, my love, that he will be coming back to you, there is a past life connection there and he will be coming back to you in either June or July. And there's something here that you had a very strong physical connection, too, quite kinky, even – because you have that passionate side to your nature and you'll want to nourish that and enjoy it. All right? Call back again if you need a longer session and to all our callers, if you want a longer session then you can give us your credit-card number and that will mean you'll be able to go beyond the twenty-minute limit.'

If she made jokes they were self-deprecating and never cruel. She giggled with another lady who wore large rings and a thick red cardigan and was also a very gifted psychic and had been all her life. Both women looked directly at the camera and smiled just enough. 'Samantha here, she was spot on, spot on. I was having trouble with a relative, quite a lot of worry and it was giving me pain in my back and my shoulder – and she told me all of that before we'd been even introduced. Didn't you?'

'And I'll be giving confidential readings for the next hour if you want to call in, if these little short readings aren't enough for you and haven't just got the detail that you need to really look at a situation and resolve it.'

They were people you could take to.

I watched for a couple of hours: the betting, the answers, the questions.

'In the spring that will be much more the way you want it. I can't tell you how, but that's going to work out and you'll be amazed, really amazed.'

Anyway, last night is why I am currently exhausted. I have no other plausible reason. And today is the first Sunday after the clocks are adjusted for spring. So you lose one hour of the sleep you didn't get and you alter your watch and your alarm and never mind the dusty leftover on your mantelpiece because it doesn't work and you can't be fussed to get it mended – it's more to look at, like a clock-shaped ornament – and after that you sit in the garden all afternoon and think there is too much light, more than an hour's worth of extra light, which is intrusive. And you spend a significant period with your self neither dreaming, nor free of night, only caught in some gap. A gap of light. The birds sing wickedly in the hedge until you bang a stick along it and send them off, the blackbirds scattering with those hard little chips of alarm, like somebody hammering at slate. I think there are nests hidden in the privet, several, and even if I am mistaken I know that the birds will return, unstoppably.

There is nothing for it but to leave the garden, the house, take a walk – for health and fitness – and in the street that loops around my garden wall it is even more clear that the new year is rising, gathering strength. The air is softer, moister, the distances changed by oncoming growth and – as you might say – the breath of seething earth, which is enough to make you feel grubby, interfered with, claustrophobic.

But I'm canny enough to avoid that and rush for the shoreline, choose the lane by the ploughed field which is barely stirring yet – the quiet, clotted one, seeds perhaps dead in it, or unwilling – and I will reach the sand and be with freshness while I pad along the beach. Silly to live so close by the sea and not take advantage.

The town catches me first, though. It's riddled with Associations and Committees, folk who set up hanging baskets for competitions, who impose their aspirations upon others. This is a place where we are supposed to think well of ourselves and of our fellow men and women and to expect the best. Which is why every lamp post I pass has a picture taped to it. Someone has lost a dog. Someone imagines that I will help them look for it, give it back if I have stolen it, apologise if I have made it into gloves. On either side of the road for as far as I can see, they've set up pictures of their missing dog.

This kind of thing is always immensely, unpardonably grim – plaintive flyers showing monochrome snaps of unrecognisable creatures that already look run over, or drowned, or vivisected, or dropped from heights. But this is worse than usual. This is tangible panic, set out on display and trying to trap me: pin-sharp colour shots of a tubby old retriever that's looking up at the camera as if it trusts me, trusts children, trusts absolutely everyone:

a few white hairs on the muzzle and sitting in a kind of happy slump surrounded by what seems a pleasant garden – much neater and bigger than mine – and signs of a pleasant existence, the kind that pleasant people would provide: people who care about animals and render them fat and unwary and who own a good computer that can print across an image in crisp, high type

MISSING
FROM THE AFTERNOON OF 21 MARCH
HE IS A MUCH LOVED FRIEND AND PET
WHOLE FAMILY WITH YOUNG
CHILDREN DEVASTATED
PLEASE HELP US WE ARE AT A LOSS

Why force me to know this? I've done nothing to them. All that detail – it's unnecessary. I can already see that the dog is a nice dog, a dog I would like if we met, and I would prefer if it wasn't lost; but I never *have* met it and I don't know where it's gone and there is nothing I can do. I am powerless in the face of these events. What purpose is served by making me feel guilty?

Beyond that, the levels of sadness involved couldn't possibly need explaining – they're what I'd assume, because I am not a psychopath, not someone entirely without imagination. Of course you don't want your dog to disappear: you feed him and love him and tend to him so that he won't. If he goes, you'll be hurt: I am fully cognisant of that. Which means you can dispense with the full-scale advertisement of household misery: dragging the kids in to make things more grisly: suggesting tears and sleepless nights and maybe – why not? – the terrible scene where Mummy, or Daddy, or possibly both, will be driven to talk with their children, however many they happen to have, and tell them all about the Facts of Death.

They will be the kind of parents who explain things and by doing this will helplessly imply that every single one of the people their children see, play with, talk to, love, may leave them without notice eternally and the truth is that huge and harmful forces stalk reality unopposed and meanwhile something shadowed and appalling may have happened to their dog, their big lovable dog with the tender muzzle and the patient eyes. They're monsters. Well-intentioned, good-hearted monsters. Their children should be rushed immediately into care.

Enough.

Much more than enough.

I take it for granted that dogs and mums and dads and children and people who have been children and the whole of the rest of everything will die and this will frequently be sudden and insupportable and unfair and in the end – no, at *my* end, the rest of the pantomime rolling on beyond me when I stop – at the end of *me* I will join them, the mysterious or rotting dead, and I am not even remotely in favour of that, but also try to never indulge such thinking unless I am overtired and lack the speed to slip out of its way. I don't want my existence to seem impractical, absurd and particularly not beyond salvation. Plus, I can't deal properly with others when all I feel is sorry they'll be leaving fairly soon and sad that so many unimportant things are so distracting.

And, then again, distraction is often exactly what I need.

The dog posters keep looking at me right along the street. Down by the crossroads he's there, too: repeating a regular perspective, unwittingly mournful in four directions. I find it impossible not to feel his household waiting somewhere close, planning further strategies. Like anyone else, they'll want to believe that effort is always rewarded.

I'd be the same.

Because it should.

Lots of dogs on the beach – unmistakable, that final pelt towards the seagrass, knowing how great it'll be when they get there, over and on to the sand, when they bark at the wave fronts, gouge the water, run themselves hoarse.

Then they come and sit beside you when they're tired. They lean against you as if two different species can communicate at certain levels and be friends. It's a nice feeling. Had it. Owned a dog when I was young. Don't exactly want to focus on that now – the long-ago, lamented companion – but naturally I am tempted because of those bloody pictures, that bloody family. *Fu-cking bas-tards.*

And the beach should be a distraction, but only if I ignore its generous and varied display of dogs and loving owners, children and loving parents, arm-in-arm loving couples, hair flaming away from them in the wind, tangling, binding. Always a good, stiff, tangling breeze when you're here, something to speed your good fortune, send it kiting. Or else the wind just blows it thin – I'd have to conduct a survey to be sure.

I see there must have been a storm. I don't remember one, nothing dramatic, but the beach is banded and heaped with dead razor shells, mussels, sea urchins, some type of delicate, pale little bivalve that I don't recognise, everything washed ashore. And a dark, new granular surface has been laid down here and there, a layer of pale grit beneath it. Signs everywhere of some great upheaval out to sea and now all this evidence of death.

Remarkable how perfect many of the shells have remained, clinking and rattling like bone when you walk in among them. I work myself deeper inside the wind, head west, away from the closed-up ice-cream huts and the people and their children and their pets. After forty minutes or so, I can be easy, be unobserved.

At the heel end of the beach everything is scoured,

flat: ghosts of dust are writhing and flaring across it at ankle height. Pebbles, sticks, shells, they balance on their own little towers of the sand they've shielded, everything else rushed to nowhere. The sun has turned unnatural, as if it's a hole punched through to somewhere white, and it's finally sinking for today, angling lower and lower until shadows are cast from almost nothing, the sand towers and fragments gaining substance, depth, beginning to look architectural, like the ruins of a city far away, miles below, deserted.

I go up and sit in the dunes and watch little gusts take a grass stem and make it write out strange calligraphy – maybe answers, or rules, promises, questions, or threats – scratched and dabbed and then worked over and then reworked, unknown word after unknown word.

Dunlins run through the shallows, too identical: tucked heads, tiny prodding beaks, pattering feet – I don't hear them patter, but at some level they must – everything the same, and then they are frightened and gather themselves to the air, barrel off.

Dusk settles, silvered at its edges and strands of red under the clouds out to sea. Which means I shouldn't be here. I'm too near the airbase and the fighters prefer to exercise when conditions become misleading, not quite day and not quite darkness. I can catch the sick tang of jet fuel from over the inlet. As I turn away the engine noise leaps and tears until it is not a sound any more, but a disturbance underfoot, in lungs, in muscles, a desire to scream while nobody will hear it.

The sunset bleeds away before I'm home.

Once I've had a bath, a thorough soaking, changed my clothes, I go into my kitchen, open up a box of spaghetti and something and then wonder what to do with it. I make a short whisky for myself, drink a mouthful and set it aside, carry myself into the bedroom and lie on the bed while the room creaks and shifts, lets go of the heat it's gathered all the afternoon. I listen while a fighter circles and heads up the coast. Another follows. They train in pairs.

I wonder if the dog is home yet. He might be. That could happen – shambling in after frolicking too long in woods, or jumping down from a benefactor's car – *We took him in a couple of days ago. Knew somebody would want him back – such a lovely old lad.* He could already be spoiled and drowsy with the big welcome he's got and the special meal and here's a new toy we bought you, just in case.

FOUND
EXACTLY WHAT WE HOPED FOR
THANKS TO EVERYONE FOR
YOUR CONCERN
WE ARE SO HAPPY NOW
NO PROBLEMS ANYWHERE

I'd like a Sunday when I see that on every lamp post. And maybe a picture of them together in the garden holding a newspaper with a date, tangible evidence that everything's okay.

I try and doze for a while with the thought of that. It's too early for sleep, but then again I'm tired.

Being this tired is tiring – which seems unjust.

'Hello?'

As usual I've picked up the phone before I'm aware it's been ringing. But there is a voice now and I can answer it. 'Hello.'

'Hi. You okay?'

My feet are cold and I'm thirsty. 'Yeah. You?' There's a little discomfort where I've lain too long on my arm.

'Been better.' His voice is cautious, a murmur.

'What time is it?'

'Not late.' I can hear that he is walking, moving through his flat – a cosy place, muffled furniture, soft fittings. 'She's gone for the week. Left the kids. So I have to mind them.' I imagine that any smashed ornaments, slivers of broken china and glass, would be tidied responsibly, quickly, in that kind of household. I assume all is in good order – good order for a place with kids. 'Where are you?'

'I'm in the bedroom.'

'Did I wake you?'

'A bit.'

'Do you want to?'

And there's a silence in which I am aware of his lips, their silk inside, relatively hot. And his hands – they are holding my voice. And I am holding his.

'If you feel like it, do you want to?'

I am walking to my living room while he speaks beside my head, my face, 'I feel like it. Of course I do. I'll just find . . .' I don't want to turn on the light, so I have to scramble about for the remote control, snatch at it because I am impatient.

'The one with the woman. Jenny? The blonde woman. I'm watching her.'

I stand in the blue attention of the television and look through our favourite channels until I find the right one. 'No, that's not Jenny. She's Tracy, isn't she? I think.' Until we're seeing the same picture.

'Jenny. Tracy . . . Are you sure you're okay? With last night?'

'Will it happen again?'

'I don't know.'

Jenny or Tracy has wigs which are not just for people with no hair. They are for fun and parties and new looks. 'Silver sand.' A man is with her and he is explaining that the wigs are extremely fine and well constructed and adds that he has known about wigs and wig technology for years and is an expert.

'Silver sand? Would you like that shade? Or the cappuccino.'

'I was on the beach today.' I change the channel and this allows me to be assured that suicide levels are down and unexplained mortality is rising. There are reasons for optimism in many areas. A chart displays the reasons as a segmented wheel.

'That's nice.' His breathing is audible, it would be touching me if it were here. 'Silver sand . . . Who is that guy with her?' He shifts position, I hear him move. 'Let's try the psychics, shall we?'

'Sure.' But I continue studying a bar chart – it has something to do with a shortage of trained personnel.

I can tell he is sitting now. He sighs and this has no colour to it, no explicit sense – it could come from tiredness, impatience, grief, 'As long as you're all right.' His hands weighted and mine too far away to lift them.

'No, I'm not all right.'

'I know, but – As long as it's as good as possible.' We have conversations when he's monotone throughout and that'll mean he's lying. On other occasions, I can hear him being playful and there's what I assume is some trick of his mother's layered in his usual melody, a light phrasing, gentle. It definitely implies a feminine influence – but not his wife's. Tonight he sounds older, as old as he'll ever get.

Myself, I sound shallow, transparent. 'Are you all right.'

'Guess.'

'I'd guess not.'

I seem to hear him rub his face, perhaps his hair. 'Yeah.' He shifts again. 'I'd guess that too.'

'Can I see you?'

'This wouldn't be a good time . . . Oh, here we go – someone who's passed is watching over the caller, well, that's nice. Or creepy. Would you want to be watched over? Dead people looking at you?'

'Probably not.'

'And in – fantastic – look at her, look at that expression, she knows she's taking the piss – in the cards there'll be an older relative who visits hospital. How unexpected is that. And it'll either be serious or not. Or maybe they won't be a patient. Christ . . .'

'Yes. Some of them aren't convincing.' I feel too much light in my head.

'People rely on crap like this. They trust it. They . . . how lost would you need to be?'

'I know.'

'I miss you.'

'Could you not say that.'

'But I do miss you.'

'And I miss you.'

This was today.

AS GOD MADE US

Dan never explained why he woke up so early, or what it was that made him leave the flat. Folk wouldn't get it if he told them, so he didn't tell. He'd just head off out there and be ready for the pre-light, the dayshine you could see at around 4 a.m. – something about 4 at this point in the year – he'd be under that, stood right inside it. Daily. Without fail. Put on the soft shoes, jersey, tracky bottoms and the baseball cap and then off down the stairs to his street. His territory. Best to think of it as his – this way it was welcoming and okay.

He'd lean on the railings by number 6 and listen and settle his head, control it, and watch the glow start up from the flowers someone had planted in these big round-bellied pots, ceramic pots with whole thick fists of blossom in them now: a purple kind and a crimson, and both shades luminous, really almost sore with brightness, especially when all else was still dim. They only needed a touch of dawn and they'd kick off, blazing. Dan liked them. Loved them. He would be sorry when they went away.

Since the birds would be more of a constant, he made sure he loved them as well: their first breaks of song across the stillness, the caution and beauty in signals that hid their location, became vague and then faded as you hunted them. He thought there was practically nothing so fine as feeling their secrets pass round him and do no harm and he'd let himself wish to hook out the notes with his fingers like smooth, hot stones: little pebbles with a glimmer he could easily hold, could picture putting in his pockets, saving them. He'd imagine they might rattle when he walked: his weight landing and swinging and landing in the way it did, the only way it could, providing enough clumsiness to jar them. Or maybe they'd call out again when they took a knock, maybe that would happen. In his head, anything could happen – it was freedom in there: big horizons and fine possibilities, that kind of balls – and chirping whenever he moved would be nice. So Dan would have it. He'd insist.

The other noises Dan could do without – there were too many of them and they were too much. They came in at him off the bare walls in his new digs, rebounded and propagated among the landlord's efforts at furniture. He'd to put up with clatters and small impacts – perhaps impacts – and vehicles – engines, metal sounds – and shouting and murmuring: voices that might be planning, that could have a bad intent, and footfalls: creeping, dashes, jogging. Fox screams were the worst – they sounded like bone pain and being lost, losing.

Caught in the house, you could not assess your situation, could neither prepare nor react – you were held in an impermissible state. Being caught at the railings wasn't as bad. Standing there you would realise that you were naked: no cover, no recourse: and so you would send a ghost of yourself running down to the basement door – send this lump from your thoughts that would chase and then lie out flat in the shadows you've seen at the foot of the steps. It could hide there, your mind between it and any harm. It could even curl up like a child, like a hiding boy, while you mother it, father it, let it be secure. The rest of you, which was the part that was real and existed and knew what's appropriate: *that* part could stay where it was and be firm – nothing going wrong – and could appreciate a mercy was taking place, a chance of survival all over again, and a measure to show your recovery's success.

This kind of trick in his thinking was needed because, as had been previously and very often discussed with professionals of several kinds, he was a brave bastard – the brave bastards being the ones who were shitting themselves and did what they had to, anyway.

He managed.

He'd begun to use earplugs when it was night. He'd be snug in his pit by ten and the covers up over his head – which made him hot, but then again he'd been hotter and covers up over would let him sleep – and the plugs would be in and packing his skull with the racket of being alive: swallowing and a background thrum – like he had engines and they were running – and his breath pacing back and forth and keeping as restless as you'd want it, keeping on.

Sometimes the press of the foam would make his ears hurt, or start to tickle, but that he could tolerate. Putting in the right one was very slightly awkward. Could be worse, though – could be having to sew on a button as part of his personal maintenance, or peeling potatoes, or that whole palaver of taking a crap – which, these days, he really noticed how often he did, even though he'd cut back on eating potatoes, obviously – except for chips from the chipper, from Frying Tonite, which were made by either Doris, or Steve, who was her other son, the one who wasn't dead. Those things were personally developmental and necessary tasks. They were interesting challenges in his reconstructed life. They were fucking pains in the arse.

When he's together with the lads he doesn't much mention such details because they are obvious and aren't important, not like they seem when he's alone.

'Oh, the many, many pains in young Daniel's delicate arse . . . But on the other hand . . .'

'On the other hand – Aaw . . . look, I dropped it.'

'Well, fucking pick it up again, hands are expensive.'

Once every month they swim together: six gentlemen sharing a leisurely day. They choose whoever's turn it is to be host, fire off the emails, travel however far, and then rendezvous at a swimming baths and christen the Gathering.

They call it that because of the movies with the Highlander in, the ones with everybody yelling at each other – *There can be only one* – and mad, immortal buggers slicing off each other's heads with these massive swords.

You have only got the one head and shouldn't lose it.

For this Gathering they'll do the usual: swimming in the morning and then a big lunch and then getting pissed and then going back to Gobbler's place, because this was his turn, and eating all his scran and some carry-out and then watching DVDs of their films and getting more pissed and maybe some porn and maybe not. They'd tried going to clubs in the early days – strip clubs, lap dancing – and one night in Aberdeen they'd gone to a neat, wee semi full of prossies – foreign prossies in fact, prossies from Moldova – but that never worked out too well. Porn was better sometimes.

In the baths everything is standard, predictable, doesn't matter what pool they come to. First there's the push or the pull on heavy doors and that walk into a thump of hot air – stuns your breath – and then chlorine smell and kiddie smell and there'll be that knowledge of a space nearby, light and high with the huge tearing windows – the windows will take out at least the one wall – and all of that water trapped underneath the airiness, that pressure and weight.

Dan and the others, they'll start mucking about, getting wound up by the anticipation of effort – flailing themselves from one place to another, hither and yon – the idea of fitness, applicable force – and more mucking about.

'Hey! Salt and vinegar!' Gobbler is shouting at Dan. Gobbler with an accent that is east of Scotland and Dan who sounds west – sounds, he supposes, like he's from Coatbridge, because he is. Gobbler is from salt and sauce land and Dan is from salt and vinegar. On occasion, they set out the subtleties of this to the others.

'Gobbler's from the heathen side – they put salt and sauce on their chips.'

'Jockanese bastards – everything's spuds with you. Like the bloody Micks.' Frank dodges in with this, yelling – sounds like he's near to Gobbler, out of sight behind a row of changing cubicles. 'How long are you meant to live, anyway, on fried Mars bars and fried pizza and fried fucking pies?'

'About till we're twenty.' Dan remembers the trip they had to Kettering – which is where Frank has settled. It's a wee, grey hoor of a place. 'Twenty years in Kettering, that'd feel like eighty. I'd top myself.'

The lot of them of them shouting back and forth at each other, scattered in the room, while they change and are overexcited and Dan thinks of being at school and how that was: swimming days with rubbish pals – pals who weren't pals at all – and not wanting to get undressed, being scared that he'd maybe sink this time, choke, scared of standing in nothing but trunks and somebody picking him out, starting something, having a go, and then the teachers coming in to the troublemakers and saying they had to behave and this being a relief to Dan, but also shaming – he knew it wasn't right, that he should sort his own problems, but couldn't. He'd been shy then and not aware of his potential and people could miss things in children – this happens constantly, he's certain – and even if an adult might try to be helpful, they might not do it a good way. Not enough care is taken. He worries for kids quite often. He wonders how they get through. He is extremely concerned that each possible kid should get through. He considers doing voluntary work with youngsters.

Dan as a youngster, he'd got his head down and tried to be correct, quiet and correct, tucked himself out of sight inside the rules. It was two years back, three, since he'd left that stuff – such a long while. He'd not forgotten, though – how he'd been useless.

Gobbler is hammering on the lockers between him and Dan and asking, bellowing, 'You got your kit off yet?' Gobbler who had another name in other times and places, when he was with other Gobblers, but now he is by himself and not in a regiment, so he is *the* Gobbler – he is the representative of his type. '*Oh, Danny Boy* . . . You having trouble?'

No one will come in and tell them they have to do anything today. They will misbehave.

'Piss off.'

'Your pants are removed over the feet, remember – not over the head. Poor bloody Paras, you do get confused.'

'Fuck off.'

And they are none of them useless.

'Are you naked yet, though, Danny? Getting hard just thinking about it.' Gobbler rattles something that sounds metallic and laughs. 'And here's old Fez, living up to his name . . . a dapper and fragrant man. Your heady aroma, sir, reminds me of those lovely evenings back at the mess when I ran the naked bar.'

A few strangers are in here too, but they are minding their own business. Mostly. Dan catches one of them giving him a walty look, in fact, the most perfectly walty look he's met: that civilian mix of need and disgust, someone who thinks he might like being scared, but wouldn't want the whole real deal, not a bit – wants to flirt, not end up being fucked. Dan stares at him while shouting back to Gobbler, shouting hard so that spittle leaves him, so that his heartbeat wakes.

'Bollocks!'

'Exactly. And where there's bollocks . . .'

'Don't start.'

'There's the mighty Gobbler javelin of Spam. You know when I get hard now —'

Everyone joining in here, because they know the words, '*It looks like I've got two dicks.*'

Gobbler's left leg gone from above the knee — which is called a transfemoral amputation — this allowing him to repeatedly assert a lie that keeps him merry, or relatively so.

There are six of them today: Gobbler, Petey, Fezman, Jason, Frank and Dan. That's two transfemoral — one with a transtibial to match — an elbow disarticulation, a transradial, a double wrist disarticulation — Frank's been hopeless at knitting ever since — and then there's Dan: he's a right foot disarticulation and a right arm transhumeral — roughly halfway between the elbow and the shoulder — the elbow which is not there any more and the shoulder which is — the elbow which Dan still feels — the elbow which is frequently wet: warm and wet, like it was when he last saw it. This is another variety of repeatedly asserted lie.

'Here we go, then. Where'd you get the trunks from, Fezman?' This from Jason who's hidden by the lockers nearest the exit.

'Girlfriend.'

'Got the DILAC trunks from his girlfriend, everyone.' When they move out for the main event, Jason will be on one side of Petey and Fezman will be on the other. They will cradle him, but won't talk about it. They will look mainly straight ahead. They will halt when they get to the footbath and threaten to dip in Petey's arse. This will make them laugh.

'He doesn't have a bloody girlfriend.' Gobbler again — a man who's fond of the chat, who probably was the same before.

Jason answers him from the footbath, 'Ah, but he's definitely got the trunks.'

'Got it the wrong way round again, Fez, you minging big window-licker. You want to have the girlfriend and fuck the trunks.'

'No. I want to fuck the *girlfriend* and *have* the trunks.'

They're all giggling, Dan can hear from every side, pissing themselves over nothing, letting themselves get daft, because that's what they want.

Gobbler's all set now for his own trip to the poolside. So, 'Come and get it then, you big Marys.'

Gobbler calls for him exactly as Dan drops his locker key, has to reach it back up, pin it to his trunks without stabbing anything precious. He removes his foot before swimming. In the thickness of the water he can feel he doesn't know it isn't there, but meanwhile he grabs on to the lockers to make his way, works himself round the houses in hops and sways like he does at home.

The other two are waiting by the time he reaches them.

Then Dan and Frank and Gobbler huddle up and start to stumble themselves along – four feet between them out of the possible six.

'Mind where you put your hand, ducky. None of that 3 Para Mortar Platoon stuff here.' Gobbler sways them too close to a wall and then back.

Dan isn't much of a talker except out on the Gatherings. 'Make your bloody mind up, Gobbler.' The rest of the time he'll maybe ask for his stop on a bus, or say something mumbly and stupid to Doris at the chipper, because she wants him to be guilty and he agrees. Probably in her mind she has the truth that there's a set amount of death and what missed Dan found someone else. She misunderstands the working of that truth, but he won't help her to figure it out. It's none of her business. 'Are you scared that *we're* gay, or are you just worried about yourself?' And Dan maybe does eat more chips than he should. 'Because we've always thought *you* were a fudge packer.' He could give them a by and not have to meet her again. 'Didn't want to say so in case you got upset.' Except she needs him to be there, he can feel that. 'You'll just end up crying and then your mascara'll run.' He needs it, too.

Frank listens and smiles down at a skinny coffin-dodger who's folding his kecks on the bench nearest to them and trying to act invisible. Frank enunciates very clearly past Gobbler's ear, 'I can give you a special handjob, help you decide – clear all your pipework.' He waggles his free stump and winks. 'Just bend over and kiss Danny's ring.'

They stagger on, holding tight, and under other circumstances it might simply be that they're drunk already and out somewhere late at night – it might be there's years not happened yet and they've some other reason for being mates.

Hospital – great place to meet folk, get new mates.

Get proper pals.

Once they're out at the pool, Dan breathes in warm and wet and is harmed by the sharp light and the din from the kids, hard noises.

A school party's here, maybe a couple – lots of primary-age heads and bodies – the water's splitting and heaving with them – all polystyrene floats and nervous piss.

Dan is aware they could prove to have an overwhelming nature, could defeat him, and he never does handle this bit too well. The panic is up and in him before he can jump and be ears full of water, wrapped by it and washed and free. He concentrates on being glad of Frank and Gobbler: the carrying, discomfort, distraction.

And he knows that once he's swimming he'll be fine. These days he goes on his back and is quite accomplished, purposeful, almost steers in the directions he intends.

'Nearly there, then.'

'Well, I had actually guessed that, you mong – cos of the fucking pool being right fucking here.' Gobbler shifts his weight and they stagger to the edge faster than intended.

Dan makes a point of exhaling and starting to grin. He is about to improve himself. He has grasped the theory, read the leaflets – people like him need a way to ignore their reminders, the signs of wounding which are their obvious and inconvenient new shape. His body is not an aid to mental rehabilitation. So he swims, makes everything glide and be jolly. This means he'll improve faster. But never as fast as he would without his injuries. That's a medical fact – if he still had his foot and the rest of his arm, he'd be finding life much better than he is.

He frowns, brings his thinking forward, peers ahead of his skin and his skull to the spot where Pete is already bobbing, hand at rest on the side and frowning up at a woman who is pacing and speaking to Fezman and Jason. They are both still dry and standing on the tiles, Fezman in these mad, knee-length trunks like he's going to play football in the 1920s but with Day-Glo palm trees and dolphins and surf on them. You can tell he fancies himself in them and they're new. They maybe are from a girlfriend.

The speaking woman is round-shouldered and wears a blouse and a long skirt so tight it almost stops her walking, only this isn't good because she has no arse, no pleasantness to see. When she angles herself and faces Dan, he ends up looking right at the curve of her little belly and her little mound and he doesn't want to. They make him sad. Everything about her is sad – browny grey and bloody depressing – hair, clothes, shoes that she clips and quarter-steps along in – and Dan can tell she's a teacher, because she's got that fakecheerful thing about her mouth and darty little eyes that are tired and want to find mistakes. Every now and then, her lips thin together and it gets obvious that her job has gone badly for her, and probably also her life. And here she is taking her class for swimming lessons on a Tuesday afternoon – for safety and fitness and possibly something else that she can't quite control. Dan is of the opinion that she should not have any kind of care over children.

'Excuse me.' The teacher doesn't speak to Dan, although she has left the others and drawn really near to him. She's maybe only in her forties, but he notices she smells of old lady.

'Excuse me.' She focuses on Gobbler. 'I realise you've been here, that you come here quite often . . .' She swallows and angles her head away, starts seriously watching the children – you'd think they were going to catch on fire, or something – not that she'd be any use to save them. 'And I've explained you to them, but now –'

'What d'you say, love?' Gobbler interrupts her and his arm around Dan flexes. 'You've explained . . . ?'

'Yes, I could explain *you* to them.'

Gobbler's arm getting ready for something, thoughts roaring about inside it, Dan can hear them.

'Don't know what you mean though, love. How you'd explain me. What you'd be explaining.' Gobbler is nearly giggling which the woman shouldn't think is him being friendly, because Dan knows he's not. 'Is that like I need translating? Like I'm a foreign language, because that's not it – British me, British to the core.'

Dan wanting to clear off out of it, avoid, and also wanting to do what he must, what he does – he goes along with the lads: Fezman, Frank, Jason, even Petey in the water, they close up alongside Gobbler, make a curvy sort of line, and they watch the woman regret herself, but still think she's in the right. 'It's the children – I know you can't help it – but they get upset.'

Dan's voice out of him before he realises, 'They don't look upset.'

'One of the girls was crying.'

'They look fine. Splashing away and happy. I mean, they do. I wouldn't say it, if they weren't.'

She tries going at Gobbler again which is unwise and Dan wonders how she managed to qualify, even get to be a teacher, when she is this thick and this shit at understanding a situation. 'I told them you were as God made you.'

'What?'

'But with so many . . . it isn't your fault, but you must see that you're disturbing.' Her hands waver in front of her, as if she can't quite bear to point at them. 'You are disturbing. I'm sorry, but you are.' She nods. 'There must be places you can go to where you'd be more comfortable.' Her fingers take hold of her wrists and cling.

And the lads don't speak.

She stays standing there and hasn't got a fucking clue.

And the lads don't speak.

Dan can tell that she has no idea they're deciding to be still, to be the nicest they can be, working up to it by deciding they will mainly forget her and what she's said and who they are.

And the lads don't speak.

She gives them a disapproving face, touch of impatience.

And Fezman nods, thoughtful, and says – he's very even, gentle with every word – says to her, 'These are new trunks. I like these trunks. They are DILAC trunks, which you don't understand.' He presses his face in mildly, mildly towards her, 'They are *Do I Look A Cunt in these trunks?* trunks and I am going to swim in them this morning. And you look a cunt and you are a cunt, you are an utter cunt and I am sorry for this, but you should know and you should maybe go away and try being different and not a cunt, but right here, right now – a cunt – you're a cunt. You are a cunt.' He nods again, slowly, and turns his face to the water and the girls and boys.

Dan watches while the woman stares and her head jumps, acts like they've spat at her, or grabbed her tits and his gone arm trembles the same way that Gobbler's does and he wants to run, can't run, wants to – wants to throw up.

The woman kind of freezes for a moment and then takes a little, hobbled step and then another, everything unsteady, leaves them.

The lads wait.

Dan sees when she reaches the opposite wall and starts yakking to a guy in a DILAC suit, guy who's standing with a Readers' Wives type of bint – they're colleagues, no doubt, fellow educators. He decides that he has no interest in what may transpire.

Dan and the lads take a breath, the requisite steps, and drop themselves into the water. They join Pete. They swim – show themselves thrashing, ugly, wild.

Dan watches the ceiling tiles pass above him and has his anger beneath him, has it pushing at the small of his back, bearing him up. It wouldn't be useful anywhere else.

And he makes sure that he watches – regularly watches out – twists and raises his head and strains to see, makes sure that the kids have cleared out of his way, out of everyone's. He wants no accidents.

In his heart, though, in his one remaining heart, there is a depth, a wish that some morning there *will* be an accident: a frightened kid, scared boy, choking and losing his way. When this happens Dan will be there and will save him.

He practises in his head and in the water – the paths that his good arm will take, the grip, the strength he's already developed in his legs.

Once that's over it will mean he has recovered himself again – become a man who would rescue a boy, who would always intend and wish to do that – would not be any other man than the man who would do that, who would be vigilant, be a brave bastard and take care.

He never would have done the thing that he couldn't have. He never would have been the man he couldn't be. He never would.

No tricks of the darkness, no sounds in the pre-light, no panic, no confusion, no walking downstairs to find it, to see how it lies like it's frightened and shouldn't be hurt. No mistake.

There should be no mistake.

There should be no mistake.

There should be no mistake.

MARRIAGE

This isn't working, he can tell.

Anybody would be able to tell.

The fact of this not working is so very obvious that he can picture it forming a cloud, an area of staining somewhere in his brain which will be exactly the colour of failure – failure being, now he thinks about it, a mix of yellow and acid green. With maybe a touch of brown. Yes, there ought to be brown. Shit brown.

Reconciliation, a ramble, pottering in shops, preparation for a smooth start to their night: none of this will happen, only the failure.

There is a little rain – dusty, irritating – and more to come, the greyness overhead creeping into their clothes, their skin, while something bruised and potentially drenching gathers above and to his left. Since they passed the library the threat of spiteful weather seems to have been tracking them, almost implausibly watchful. And her shoulders are already locked in that depressive-looking flinch away from him. The usual.

So they won't have a giggle. They won't be companions. They won't chat. They will just walk, trudge on. She will trash their afternoon.

Her feet will continue to bang down with a rhythm that is not his own, that doesn't even seem quite hers. She will beat up ahead of him, striding out for that full yard of distance, keeping it wedged in between them. She likes making him study her back – a back which

127

grows more eloquent the longer he stares at it. Currently, it is both wounded and resentful – in another half an hour it will be martyred and she will be an icon of patient suffering. He realises he has already started shrugging at passers-by to offset her effects. Any especially interested strangers are offered a little purse of the lips, a slight raising of his eyebrows, suggesting something along the lines of –

My wife – you have to love her, eh? Well, I have to, anyway. She's temperamental, you might say. A bit overbred. Still, we weather the storms. Oh, indeed we do. Both of us. Here we are. Weathering.

Or sometimes he droops his head, the well-disciplined husband, peers out at possibly like-minded gents.

In the doghouse again, then. Silly me.

A few streets ago, she raised her pace and she's still rushing. She's not *running*, though: nothing as frank and outgoing as that, and nothing casual or girlish, she won't break into a trot – she is a subtle woman and has settled for a kind of driven scamper, because this will disturb him most. She is forcing her body to seem endangered, animal, and draws him on behind her into a state of contagious despair. He feels himself caught in the movements of an anxious man: pursuing, pursued, escaping, arriving too late for essential – but undefined – aid, losing support.

Not that I ever am late. That's her trick. Punctual, me. Punctual parents – that's what sees you right. Conditioned before you know it and, as a result, you're courteous. Whenever you're needed, you're already there.

He folds his hands into his pockets – soft flannel lining, warm.

The flannel there at his request.

My request.

My coat.

It's a consolation. The only piece of clothing that he's

ever had made. Bespoke. Specifically cut and fitted for his shoulders, his arms, his back, the touch of it against him like a light embrace, something manly, brotherly. She'd remarked on its cost at the time, of course, couldn't help herself. At least, she'd looked at him and never even smiled while he told her about this amazing little old-fashioned shop he'd found and the bolts and bolts of tweed they had inside and the remarkable, genuinely surprising, lack of expense about it all if you considered the work involved and the fact that such an overcoat would last a lifetime, very easily a lifetime. She had simply shaken her head at him as if he'd been fooled, as if advantage had been taken. Which meant that he'd not had a chance to mention the tailor – *his* tailor – the pallid and serious face, the deft hands as they measured, the voice so very certain and precise as it rattled off a pattern of numbers to an assistant – his tailor had an assistant – and marked out the code to record a form, to recall it and set everything snug with it. And he didn't, until later, make a point of describing the atmosphere of complete civility.

Not fawning, nobody likes that – they just had a proper way of seeing. They saw me. I gave them my time, they studied, paused for thought, and then they understood the way I want to be, the way I really ought to be. They surprised me with myself.

First fitting, and the man there in the mirror, he's wearing a big coat, a long coat, something with personality, something to draw attention. He's standing well, firmly, so the cloth hangs as it should. He doesn't fidget, doesn't have to, he meets my eyes – no staring, only confidence, interest, calm. I like him. I like myself.

My better self.

My better whole self.

I'm not that tall, not striking, but they knew – the shop folk were sure I could carry it off. My coat.

*I didn't ask for any changes, only let them refine their work
– chalk and pins and whispers – let them give me this one
thing which is absolutely as it should be.*

Nice to be able to redefine what you deserve.

While she scurries on ahead, he feels the coat clap at
his shins, its weight pressing and cuddling around him.
Serious weather shows it off to advantage, naturally.
Breezes sleek it against him, or flare it wide. Rain lets
him turn up his collar as he did when he stepped outside
this morning, a part of his mind dipping quickly through
into a finer, much more elegant world of couples whose
romances started on ocean liners, or cross-country trains:
careless and witty people who solve mysteries, sing in
nightclubs, only fight before falling much harder and
deeper back into love.

He and his wife were not falling, not anywhere.

They were walking – had been for hours, further and
further into the Saturday mess of downtown. They hadn't
gone according to his hopes, hadn't stopped for lunch,
hadn't taken the tiny ferry, knees tucked together on the
fibreglass bench, hands touching as they bobbed across
the inlet, swung above a jaunty depth, the push and clap
and swell. They hadn't bought lunch on the island: a
lobster apiece and melted butter, or Dungeness crabs,
something messy and tasty and special. They hadn't simply
chosen apples from the market hall, those organic ones
that taste particularly healthful – *Ambrosia? Nectar?* –
they've some pseudo-religious name, but he can't quite
place it. Just a bag of apples that have nothing wrong
about them and smell clean, it would have been good
to hold that.

He'd wanted to give her a splendid day, but she wouldn't
listen, wouldn't agree, wouldn't let him take her hand,
wouldn't stop chasing from street to street, crossing where
she shouldn't, darting out between moving cars. And he
had to follow. For a few blocks she'd picked a run of

alleyways: abandoned pallets, bins of food waste, furtive doorways, the stink and the threat of feral activities. He wondered if the impulse was self-destructive, or if it was him she intended to be destroyed.

These last few months, he couldn't tell what she intended. Back at home, their rooms were almost emptied, only necessary items still in place, two new walls of filled boxes in the hallway. By the end of Monday he'd be gone, enjoying the change of setting, the extra space, and wanting her to like it, too – wraparound balcony and not a bad view of the park. Going up in the world. She'd told him that she was excited by the move, but then she'd filled up those bags with her clothes – a good deal of her clothes, most of them – fussed through one entire evening and then put them out to be thrown away. All right, she'd lost weight lately, some of the blouses, skirts, they might not still fit, but even so – and she never did explain it, her motivation, this desire to sacrifice.

Or else she was hoarding – that was her other extreme. There was the time he'd caught her opening a finished box, cutting its tape, sliding an ugly little coffee cup with its saucer in among the packing, 'They're Victorian.' Accusation in her voice, when all he'd done was head across the corridor and happen to notice her, this was before he'd said a word.

'They're Victorian and hideous.' Which they were, he was being factual with that.

'They were my mother's.'

'I've never seen them before.'

'I know.' Glancing up at him as if she were at bay, as if his seeing them would harm them, make them even more violently painted and chipped than they already were.

And she'd closed the box over again with this dreadful, melodramatic slowness, plastered new tape across it, binding the wound in the cardboard – that's what it looked like – binding a wound and guilt. He'd been bewildered – no, astonished – astonished was the better word, when he described the scene to his friends he would say *astonished*. No use talking to her, as ever – he'd just gone and sat up on the kitchen counter, opened a beer. Warm beer, the fridge defrosting, small detonations of ice beside his head. He'd wriggled his feet in the air, breathed slowly, tried to drop right back into enjoying how soon they would leave and the way that took his every action here and made it light.

And the austerity of his home as it was – boxed, packed, stripped – he appreciated that. Their bedroom, for example, had nothing left in it but the bed. Ghosts and traces on the carpets, the walls, where belongings once belonged, but now there was the bed and no more. Last night this had seemed remarkably fine for a while – his room, his wife, his bed. It had been an invitation. He'd walked into the dark and let it tease him, heat him, as he padded from the doorway, all the naked surfaces giving him echoes as he moved, enlarging everything he did into wonderful shocks, each sound like a break, a snap, a slap.

I don't know where she's going.

I don't believe that she does either.

His wife has reached a series of concrete barriers, chain-link fence, and beyond them an artificial chasm where the city is digging out foundations for a new railway line. The construction work has sealed off cross streets and gouged out blocks of the road it seems she had wanted to follow.

So maybe she did have a purpose.

Or maybe she's only confused.

She could be lost.

That's not too improbable. Or else she's worn out and a touch bewildered, overwrought.

Me, too.

132

He could close on her, stand at her shoulder, but he chooses not to because this might upset her more and perhaps lead them into some kind of disturbance. Other pedestrians, he notices, quite often glance at her, but never smile or speak. They won't engage her, either. Also, although he has kept his distance from her and has, for hours, made no sign that he even knows this woman ahead of him, still no one has drifted into the space between them, no one has intervened. He finds that strange.

She starts off again, much slower. He ambles along in her wake, rounding the blunt end of the site and then tracking along beside the line of fencing, the warning signs, the sunken din. As she goes, she is peering through and down to look at the excavation and he can see her face, her right cheek and eye.

I felt it that time.

For sure.

Jarred me in the forearm.

She forgets that I'm left-handed sometimes, ducks the wrong way.

Other times she doesn't see it coming.

And to be fair, he rarely hits her in the face – it isn't something she'd expect.

But in that bedroom – so hungry, empty, blinded out around him – what's there was purely, truly exactly his – what was needed – pinned back to the essential – she is his wife, she is married to him – she was there in his home, in his room, in his bed in his dark and supposed to be his love – the feel of her smile, he was trying for that, his mouth idiotic with trying to find out that, with expecting her to be alive for him – but she turned away, she turned her back – this endlessly, endlessly cold, stupid bitch – just turned her back.

Oh, in the end, she let him – eventually she let him – lying like meat and he's being *allowed* – he's being *allowed* – his own wife.

So he stopped.
Pulled out and stopped.
Hanging.
Damp.
Hot.
Breath so loud in his head.
Hit her.
Just the once.
The noise of it.
Fantastic.
Like a shot.
Came after that.
Back in her and came.
Like a shot.
Which is why she had to be so awkward about today.

She's halted, her right hand with its palm pressed flat against the fence, three fingers hooked through the links, tensed. Because it finally feels possible to do this, he paces slowly in towards her, stops near enough for the cloud of her breath to reach him. Below there are two men with shovels standing on what appears to be fragmented shale. It is the same clotted purple and grey as the sky, or perhaps it is only wet and is somehow reflecting the sky for a while, but is, in itself, much less impressive. There is anyway something odd, he thinks, about all of this – shovels seem old-fashioned for such a modern undertaking, a high-speed rail link, an urban showpiece. The rock there odd, too – this echo of the sky discovered underfoot and three or four storeys of digging to reach it, to expose something so secret, so permanent, that it shudders the city round about him, the laughable buildings, the slow damage that is inside everything.

Beneath them, the metal shovels grate as they're driven into the loosened stones, gather them up.

She starts to cry. 'I don't know how they stand it.' No fuss. Soft weeping.

Together they watch the two men work under the rain. Every time the blades bite home there is a mineral squeal, a sense of historical weight.

She repeats herself more quietly, 'I don't know how they stand it.'

And he covers her hand with his and draws her round to him, against him. There is a tremor in her arms and back, but he holds her tight enough to quiet it and lets her press the unharmed part of her face against his chest and hovers his fingers over the harmed but does not touch it, because he understands it is there and that is enough.

'They stand it fine.'

And he brushes the warm of her hair, cradles her head and then winds both arms around her, stills her: the shape of his coat, he imagines, bringing more than a dash of romance to the scene. They will be admired, a little focus of attention for the street. And everyone who sees them will be sure – this is what it looks like. This is exactly what it looks like. Marriage.

STORY OF MY LIFE

In this story, I'm like you.

Roughly and on average, I am the same: the same as you.

The same is good. The same is that for which we're meant. It's comforting and gently ties us, makes us unified and neat and it tells us the most pleasant kinds of story, the ones that say how beautifully we fit, the ones that summon up their own attention, make us look.

I understand this.

I understand a lot – very often – almost all the time – most especially the stories. They are an exercise of will: within them whatever I think, I can wish it to be. They are the worlds that obey me, kinder and finer worlds: in many of them, for example, I'd have no teeth.

Because I believe I'd do better with a beak. So why not have one? That shouldn't be impossible. I feel a beak could make me happy, quite extraordinarily content: sporting something dapper and useful in that line – handy for cracking walnuts, nipping fingers, tweezing seeds. Not that I've ever fancied eating seeds, but one can't predict the path of appetite.

And beaks come in different sizes: that's a plus, along with the range of designs. The toucan would be good for parties, shouting, grievous bodily harm. Ibis: mainly funerals and plumbing. Sparrow: best for online dating and eating crisps. The options, while not infinite, are extensive. In a reasonable world my personality would give rise to my true beak, would nurture it, my proper fit – parrot, hummingbird, bullfinch, albatross – and through it I'd express myself, be jauntily apparent, fulfilled, really start going somewhere with my whole appearance – somewhere free from teeth – somewhere other than the dentist.

Story of my life – maybe – going to the dentist.

Because my teeth, they've always been ambitious, problematic, expansive. I never have had enough room for all of them and so out they've come: milk teeth, adult teeth, wisdom teeth: handfuls of them over the years, practically a whole piano's worth. Of course, when I was a kid they still gave you gas for extractions – general, potentially fatal, anaesthetic gas administered, in my case, by an elderly man with unhygienically hairy ears who would bend in at me, eerily grinning, and exclaim – every single time – 'Good Lord, dearie, they're some size, those teeth,' while he flourished that black rubber mask and then cupped me under it, trapped my mouth in one hard, chilly pounce: 'Breathe deeply, dearie. Count backwards from ten.'

I'd shut my eyes and picture his tufted, werewolf earlobes and count until I'd reached as far as seven or so before I'd see these angles of tilting grey that folded in towards a centre point, bolted and sleeked at the backs of my eyes and then rolled me down and away to the dark.

Now, as it happens, I'm not good with chemicals. No choice here – I am made the way I'm made. Sensitive.

In the chair they'd give me nitrous oxide and it put me out nicely enough. I'd swim deep through a cartoony, bendy blank while the dentist did his work – the tugging, the twists – then I'd float straight back up and just bob at the surface like a tiny shore-leave sailor: changeable and land-sick and absolutely smashed.

My first experience of the freedom within incapacity.

That swoop and rock and thunder of delight. It's always best to meet your pleasures before you can tell what they mean.

As I came round some nurse would be attending with her kidney dish and towels: a bit broody perhaps, protective – the motherly type but not a mother and therefore idealistic, if not ridiculous, about kids. She would, shall we say, not entirely expect the violence of my post-operative dismay: my tiny swinging fists and my confusion, my not unjustifiable sense of loss.

I have no idea what I shouted on these occasions – a small person turning expansive, losing it, throwing it, swarming clear out into beautiful rage. I'll pretend, while I tell you the story, that I know.

I'll say I produced – at great speed and with feeling – 'You get away from me! I'll have you! I'll set the Clangers on you. And Bagpuss! Taking my teeth out . . . no one ever takes *me* out – except to the dentist – to take out more teeth. I need my teeth for the Tooth Fairy – I'm only five, for Chrissake – that's my one source of income, right there. How else can I save up to run away from here? I could go on the stage – be a sideshow – my manager would want me absolutely as I am – *the Shark Tooth Girl: the more you pull, the more she grows: ivory from head to toes*. I'd be laughing. With all of my teeth, I'd be laughing.'

This is untrue, but diagnostic – it helps to make me plain.

Because I wouldn't ever want to hide from you.

The surprise of my own blood, that's true – thick and live and oddly tasty – I never did get used to that, my inside being outside – on my face, my hands. Even today, if I take a tumble, suffer a lapse, my blood can halt and then amaze me. It's almost hypnotic – seeing myself run. And persons of my type, we run so easily: birds' hearts thumping in us and broad veins full of shocks.

Back from the surgery, next came the hangover – naturally, naturally, naturally – but as I was a child it would be kind, more a mild type of fog than a headache. Beyond it I'd be given soldiers with boiled eggs, gentle food for an affronted mouth and a sudden hunger – oh, such a lively hunger – and a quiet mother comfort to meet it with a little spoon. Then a bath and an early night pelting with lurid dreams of thieves and tunnels and running for my life, right through my life and out the other side and into nowhere: the coppery taste of absence, liquid heat.

Once I was older, I decided I had no more time to waste – people to do and things to be – and avoiding the dental issue became attractive. I brushed regularly, kept my head down, ate everything wholemeal for added wear, but it did no good: my teeth are forceful. They insist.

So when I'm twenty-four, twenty-five, I'm back in the surgery – new dentist – and the first of my wisdom teeth is leaving. Local anaesthetic this time, much more practical and safe, and I haven't enjoyed the injections, but I'm hoping they'll do the trick – mostly my eye's gone a little blurry, but that's nothing to fret about – and here comes the dentist – big man, meaty forearms, substantial grip – and it's plain that he'll check now, tap about to see if I'm numb and therefore happy – except he doesn't. He does not.

And I should pause here briefly, because it lets the story breathe and even possibly give a wink. I step back to let you step forward and see what's next. This way you'll stay with us. With me.

Which is the point.

You staying with me is the point.

And, no, the dentist doesn't check, he is incurious and generally impatient, goes at it fiercely with the pliers and no preamble and here comes a clatter, a turning yank, and then tooth – I am looking at my tooth without me, grinning redly in the light – and I am puzzled because of this feeling, this building feeling which I cannot quite identify – it is large, huge, and therefore moving rather slowly, takes a full *count backwards from tennineeight* to arrive and then I know, then I am wholly, supernaturally aware, I am certain in my soul that I'm in pain. This is hitherto unguessed-at pain – pain of the sort I have tried to anticipate and forestall with insulating activities and assistance. Numb is best – I always aim for numb, for numb of any type – but pain has found me anyway. Worse than imagination, here it is.

To be fair, the dentist was upset – looking down at me and saying, 'Oh, dear,' a number of times before offering a seat in his office and an explanation involving wrongly positioned nerves – it was technically my fault for having provided them. His secretary gave me a comforting and yet excruciating cup of tea.

I walked home – it wasn't far – dizzy and racing with adrenalin. They put it in the anaesthetic, presumably to give it extra zip. Which is to say that you go to the dentist – somebody worrying – and he then injects you with terror – pure fear – you feel it rush your arms, cup its lips hard over that bird inside your chest.

And it is possibly, conceivably, odd that this is so familiar, so really exactly the simple jolt of many mornings and you draw near to your house and wonder, as usual, if so much anxiety should not have a basis in fact. Perhaps a leak under your floorboards has caused rot, perhaps you're ill – genuinely threatened by what, as soon as they knew you weren't suing, your dentist and his secretary called *a head injury* – this making you feel very noble for not complaining, but nevertheless, in many ways it sounds dire. And if you really want to fret, then perhaps you shouldn't lend that guy your money – your guy, your money, but shouldn't they still be apart? You like them both but they should surely be apart? And what if he isn't exclusively your guy, you've had that unease, felt that whisper, about him before – and it's screaming today. And what if your life is, in some degree, wrong or maladjusted when hauling a live tooth raw from the bone leaves you and your state no worse than an average night, a convivial night, a pace or two along your path of joy.

Sensitivity, you see? It causes thoughts.

When I reached the flat, I let myself in and sat on the sofa, hands holding each other to dampen their shake and keep out the sense of having gone astray: twenty-five and no real profession, no prudent strategy, not much of a relationship.

And too many teeth.

But you try to keep cheery, don't you? And you have time. At twenty-five you've bags of it.

Thirty-five, that's a touch more unnerving – wake up with thirty-five and you'll find that it nags, expects things you don't have: kitchen extensions and dinner parties, DIY, the ability to send out Christmas cards signed *With love from both of us. With love from all of us.*

Instead I'm house-sitting for friends.

And this section of the story is here for you to like and to let your liking spread to me. Frailty and failure, they're charismatic, they have a kind of nakedness that charms.

So.

Minding the house is company for me.

Well, it *isn't* company – the owners are obviously away, hence my minding – and they've left their cats. And this is domesticity without effort: Brazilian cleaning lady, leather cushions, large numbers of superfluous and troubling ornaments.

This isn't like me owning cats, me living alone with cats, me growing six-inch fingernails and giggling through the letter box when the pizza-delivery man comes, peering out at him and smelling of cats – that's not how it is.

There are these other people who are not me and they are the ones who have the cats and I am treating their animals politely but with an emotional distance, no dependency and no indications of despair. There should be no suggestion that these friends are sorry for me, that the husband is more sorry than the wife and that they have argued about my trustworthiness in their absence and their possessions and have doubted the supervisory skills of a Portuguese-speaking obsessive-compulsive who polishes their every surface twice a week: tables, glasses, apples, doorknobs, the skin between the end of the air and the beginning of my wine. I will not tell you they left behind them a plethora of mildly hysterical notes, or that their act of charity has been overshadowed by a sense of filth, oncoming sadness.

It is only important to mention that I was, on this particular house-sitting evening, chipper and at ease. I had fed both of the creatures and I was going out – out on a date – a variation on a theme of what could be a date. We had reached a transitional stage, the gentleman and I – which is to say, I had reached it and wondered if he had too – and I have to make the best of what I may get, so I was dressed presentably and poised to be charming and, had it not been for the stitches in my mouth, I would have been perfectly on form.

More dentistry – surgical dentistry, but with mouthwash and antibiotics and painkillers – big ones.

I like them big.

So I'm all right.

I'm stylish.

And I slip into the restaurant – once I've found it – with what I consider to be grace and it's an agreeable establishment. Italian. So I can have pasta – which is soft.

And here's my date – my approaching a date – and he's looking terrific.

He's looking great. Like a new man.

Truly amazing.

He's looking practically as if he's someone else.

Yes.

Yes, he is.

He is someone else.

I am waving at someone else. The man I am meeting is sitting behind him and to the left and not waving. No one, to be accurate, *is* waving apart from me and I would love to stop waving, but have been distracted by the expression on my almost-date's face.

He is experiencing emotions which will not help me.

But I can still save the evening. I'm a fighter. I calmly and quietly explain the particular story which is presently myself: the drugs I am currently taking – prescribed drugs – the residual levels of discomfort, the trouble I have enunciating – and perhaps he might like to tell me about *his* week and I can listen.

People like it when you listen.

They have stories, too.

But he doesn't give me anything to hear.

And so I talk about my roots – *that* story – a little bit angry, because he should have been better than he is, should have been a comfort. My roots are 23 millimetres long, which is not unimpressive, is almost an inch. I tell him about my root canals. I summarise the activities involved in an apesectomy – the gum slicing, tissue peeling, the jaw drilling, the noise.

This is not romantic, because I no longer wish to be, not any more. I am watching a space just above his head and to the right where another part of my future is closing, folding into nowhere, tasting coppery and hot.

Could be worse, though: could be forty-five, when everything tilts and greys and comes to point behind your eyes and you have not run away, you have waited for the world to come towards you, given it chance after chance. And, besides this, you find it difficult to name what else you have done, or who is yours. After so many years you are aware of certain alterations, additions, the ones that would make you like everyone else, that would join you, tie you gently, allow you to fit.

But they don't make a story – they're only a list.

More dental adventure, that'll keep us right – another practice, another extraction, another tale to tell and that remaining wisdom tooth: it's shy, it lacks direction, the time has come to cut it out.

Cheery dentist, in this instance, talkative, 'This is an extremely straightforward operation. It is, of course, *oral surgery* but you'll be fully anaesthetised.' Which is frankly the least I would hope – and dialogue, that's always a boon – a voice beyond my own, someone in whom I can believe.

He puts his needle in, 'There we are . . .' and the numbness goes up to my eye. Again. Faulty wiring. So my mouth is now more painful than it was and I'm also half blind. 'Well, I'll just deal with that, then – there you go.'

Oh, that's better, that is good. Thass gread.

And this is my speaking voice, my out-loud voice, the one for everyone but you. *So it's in italics* – that way you'll know.

Thass bedder. Thass suffithiently aneasssetithed. You may protheed.

When we're in private – like now – and I say this to no one but you, then italics are unnecessary.

We can be normal and alone.

'No, I think you need more than that.'

And this is where the dentist gives me more anaesthetic and I notice his hands smell a little like cornflakes – his gloves, they have this cornflaky scent – which is a detail that makes him seem credible and not simply a nightmare.

'Perhaps a touch more there.'

Whad? No, no thass a bid mush.

'And some more.'

Shurly nod?

'And more than that. Splendid.'

I can'd feed by arms.

'Of course, the effects of the anaesthetic will usually pass after three or four hours. But working so close to a nerve, as we will, in very unusual patients the numbness will pass in three or four . . .'

It would be tiresome to pause here.

So we won't.

'. . . months and in some extraordinary cases, you will be like that . . .

'. . . for the rest of your life.'

Unf?

'Here we go then.'

It's not that I don't appreciate the chance to feel nothing at all – but this isn't that – this is horror combined with paralysis – only very minutely exaggerated paralysis. I can't see to hit him, I can't fight him off and he's digging and drilling, drilling and digging and the extraction takes forty-five minutes.

Honestly.

That's how long it takes – no exaggeration.

There's blood in his hair.

It's mine.

Finally, I'm released, it's over, the stitches have been stitched, and I run out of the surgery.

Well, I pay the bill and I run out of the surgery.

Well, I pay the bill and ask them to call me a cab and I run out of the surgery.

Well, I can't really run, but I leave the surgery as best I can and I wait for the cab in what happens to be a colourful urban area, one where relaxed gentlemen stroll the boulevards of an afternoon and possibly sing. Perhaps there may be vomit on a lapel here and there. Perhaps there may be vomit and no lapel. And I'm standing – just about – and I can hear a relaxed gentleman coming along behind me.

He says something approaching, 'Hhaaaaa.' Which is not much of a story, but is true and I know what he means because I can speak alcoholic. I have learned.

He reaches me and he says what might be expected – 'Scuse me cunyou spare twenny pence furra cuppa tea?' And I turn to him with my bleeding mouth and my lazy eye and my dodgy arm and my swollen tongue and I say, 'I don no. Havin a biddofa bad day mysel.'

So he gave me twenty pence.

And a slightly used sweet.

And a kiss.

It's best, if you can, to close up every story with a kiss. If you can.

Story of my life – maybe – going to the dentist.

The story that kept you here with me and that was true. In its essentials it was never anything other than true.

True as going to sleep tonight with the idea of blood beneath my tongue and meeting the old dreams of robbery and tunnels, the ones where I run straight through and beyond myself and on. And sometimes I wake up sore and wanting to set out nice fingers of bread and runny egg and avoiding the issue is always attractive, but I am tired of speaking languages that no one understands and I have only these words and no others and this makes my stories weak, impossible – impossible as the Christmas cards – *with love from all of us* – the night hugs and pyjamas, the tantrums and the lost shoes and the hoarding of eccentric objects: figurines, sea glass, washers: which are the kind of details that should not be discussed. They are impossible as hiding the so many ways that my insides leak out, show in my hands, my face.

Impossible as telling you a story of a new arrival – a small person, turning expansive – someone growing and beautiful, but not perfect, the story of their first trip to the dentist, their first real fear I'd want to drive away. My duty would be to ensure that we would conquer, because every pain is survivable, although it may leave us different, more densely ourselves. The child and I, we would be unafraid and we'd have stories and every one of them would start with

In this story, you are not like me.

All of my life I'll take care we are never the same.

SYMPATHY

'Is this wise?'

'Sorry?'

'I said – *is this wise?* Which is . . . I just didn't want a silence – not right now. I think. Nervous.'

'So you're making conversation.'

'Maybe. Clearly not managing that well . . . I should ask, though – is this wise?

'Do you want it to be?'

'Come here a minute. If you're just going to stand over there I'll get lonely. Need a cuddle.'

'Need more than that, I hope. I wanted to draw the curtains. So you can turn on the light.'

'So we can see.'

'So we can see. And so here I am.'

'God, you smell nice. And feel nice. And the lady doesn't want the curtains open, but a strange man . . . in her hotel room . . . that's fine.'

'Are you a strange man?'

'You don't know me.'

'But I don't think you're strange.'

'You're not scared?'

'Do I look scared.'

'No.'

'Do you want me to look scared.'

'No. Not really. But you can keep doing that. Bit higher. Bit lower. Perfect.'

'Like Goldilocks and the beds. Or the porridge. Which would you rather be – porridge or bed?'

'Guess.'

'Wouldn't really be a guess, though, would it. More like stating the obvious.'

'That I'm clearly a man for porridge?'

'Exactly . . . And meanwhile there's being strange and then there's being a stranger. You being a stranger – that's kind of the point, isn't it?'

'Is it?'

'And you look all right.'

'Thanks a lot.'

'I mean safe.'

'Thanks a hell of a lot.'

'Okay, you look like I'm going to fuck you. And you're going to fuck me. How's that.'

'That's . . . true. And so I should . . .'

'Where are you going?'

'Put my coat over the chair – if it's on the floor I'll think about it being on the floor . . . I'm tidy.'

'And nervous.'

'Yeah. Why not . . . Your beauty renders me nervous . . . and you don't look like a strange woman. In case you were about to ask.'

'How can you tell – Rose West didn't look like a strange woman.'

'Yes, she did. And she looked fat. *Was* fat.'

'You have a problem with fat women?

'Are you likely to get fat between now and tomorrow morning?'

'I'll try not.'

'Then I don't have a problem. That's a nice arse. Neat little skirt, neat little arse . . . but you've trashed your room. Messy. Now why's that? Are you messy? Messy and a neat arse. Going to want to get to know that arse.'

'I wasn't expecting you.'

'Well, no. I wouldn't think you were.'

'I wasn't expecting anyone. So I didn't tidy. Nice suit.'

'Yeah, I scrub up well. Or else I'm like this all the time, let's say I'm like this all the time. That's sad. Not my suit – my suit isn't sad. It's sad that you weren't expecting anyone . . . And how are you finding me so far? How am I doing?'

'What, you want marks for technique?'

'Sure. Why not. Maybe I have a notebook and I keep score.'

'In that case . . . it feels as if you've kissed people before.'

'In a good way?'

'Like you've practised. Done a module. Or you have a notebook and keep score.'

'I don't have a notebook. You do have very beautiful lips, though. I thought that – first thing I thought.'

'What do you smell of?'

'Ahm, I don't know . . . Soap, mainly. Posh soap they give you here . . . Maybe my dinner – I had lamb. I don't think I spilled any on my shirt . . . Gravy? I probably smell of gravy and the inside of a hired Nissan Micra . . . and manliness . . .'

'Manliness . . . Well, I like it, anyway, whatever it is – how your skin smells . . . What about Crippen?'

'Hm?'

'Dr Crippen – he looked normal.'

'Scary glasses.'

'Dr Shipman.'

'Scary beard. I had a beard once. Would you have preferred that?'

'No. John Wayne Gacy?'

'He dressed as a clown.'

'He *was* a clown.'

'That's no excuse. Were you thinking of dressing as a clown?'

'I never travel with the costume – shoes are too big for my bag. D'you want to do that again.'

'What, this?'

'Yeah. That.'

'Or how about this?'

'That too.'

'This isn't something I normally do, though. In fact. In case you were wondering.'

'You don't normally put your hands up women's skirts?'

'Not women I haven't . . . met before. What about you?'

'I don't fancy women.'

'Seriously, though, I don't ever. Until this.'

'Haven't ever fucked a stranger.'

'You do like the stranger thing, don't you? Gets you going. Gets you. It gets you that you don't know my name, won't know it – how's that? Oh, you like that. And you don't know where my hands have been – if I've washed them – and where's that finger going to go. Like that too, don't you? Don't even know my name and I'll never know yours . . . We're lucky – paths crossing – I'm not in hotels that much. Hardly ever. I had to . . . hold on, I think I should . . . we don't really need my jacket any more, do we?'

'I think we should get on with this, yes.'

'Okay, okay . . . But I'll hang it up then, if that's . . . here we go – Jeez, they don't give you many coat hangers, do they? The price you're paying for the room, you'd think there'd be more. Can I put it over this blouse?'

'Why would I worry what you put your jacket over?'

'I was being polite. Polite stranger.'

'Sorry. Come back and be polite with me.'

'Having sex doesn't mean I needn't be polite. Even when I'm being rude I can be polite. That's why, as you will notice, I'm removing both my shoes and my socks. A gentleman always removes his socks . . . Folds his trousers . . . Thus . . . Thuswise . . . Anyway . . . Hotels . . .

Yeah, I had to get condoms out of the vending machine in the Gents. Indicating I don't travel with them.'

'Or indicating you've run out. Might have been a busy week.'

'I'm not like that. I'm just right now saying that I'm not like that.'

'Well, neither am I.'

'I know, I know . . . I can tell. It's just a nice . . . idea. And we can be like this tonight.'

'Eventually.'

'All good things to those who are patient and have a nice arse. Fruit flavour's all they had left – in the condoms. Sorry. And here's me, back again. Barefoot and no more jacket, no more suit. Hi.'

'Hello.'

'D'you like my boxers. Sorry about the rather obvious hard-on.'

'No, you're not.'

'No, I'm not. D'you want to take anything off?'

'Pick.'

'Take off my tie.'

'What?'

'I'd like you to take off my tie – maybe I like the taking off the tie thing, the way you like the stranger thing. And if I have to choose your sweater or your skirt, I'd probably go for the skirt. So you can take that off, too. Please. And undo my buttons. Do you like being told what to do?'

'Not the way you mean it.'

'Thank Christ for that – I'd really rather not be in charge. It's been a long week, as it happens – and we're only on Wednesday . . . Not a bad week, but . . . long. You going to take your skirt off, or not?'

'Kiss me.'

'Absolutely. I aim to please . . . What about your skirt?'

'It's coming.'

'And are you? . . . Sorry. Not funny. Not clever . . . It's always . . . this bit's tricky . . . Fuck, that's nice, though. That's . . . that's lovely. That's . . . an eyeful. Only a eyeful's . . .'

'A tower?'

'Something off a seaside postcard. *Ooh, missus, what an eyeful* . . . Then again, under the sweater, I'll bet . . . there's another. Such a lot of good things you have about you. I love you.'

'No you don't.'

'But I want to say I do. And let's see if I can . . .'

'If you want to unfasten it, then unfasten it – don't just fiddle with it . . . What bit's tricky? The catch?'

'No. That's . . . fine. It's this bit. You know – we're not completely started, but we're not completely – oh, you could do that some more, actually – not completely carried away yet. It's like being thirteen – makes me feel awkward.'

'I was thinking it was like being fifteen. But you started early, did you?'

'I started on my own.'

'Start, finish, it's all on your own.'

'Don't say that.'

'How am I now? Better?'

'Let me look, then.'

'You are looking.'

'I know. Gorgeous.'

'Liar.'

'Why don't you think you're beautiful.'

'I was joking.'

'No you weren't. Fuck – legs all the way up to here. Right. Here. Fuck. I've just realised – I like saying fuck to you. *Fuck*. FUCK!'

'Shhh.'

'What for.'

'They'll hear you – in the other rooms.'

'Which you'll like. Strangers hearing you fuck a stranger. FUCK! ME!'

'Then don't just say it.'

'Does that feel like I'm just going to say it? Does it?'

'Because, if we keep talking, we're going to end up –'

'Getting to know each other?'

'That wouldn't work.'

'Fine.'

'Well, don't sound annoyed.'

'I'm not annoyed.'

'You are.'

'Take off your knickers.'

'Ah, I . . . Could you? Please? Would you like to?'

'Look, I don't know if . . .'

'What? . . . What's wrong?'

'Take them off yourself.'

'What's wrong?'

'Take them off. *Now.* Do it. Okay. *Good.* And here's what we do. Okay? This is when you get what you want. Okay? You get exactly what you're asking for. So now shut up and show me your tits. Really. I mean it. I'm very serious. Hold them. Together. And squeeze. Harder. You don't know me, we've never met, so I have to explain – *I need to see your tits.* Show me. And open your legs. Right open, you're not shy, you want this. And touch it. Touch it. If you want this, you won't be shy. You'll like it. You'll touch yourself and show me everything. Relax and *show me.* That's it. Just relax. Like it. Because this is what you like and twenty . . . I make it twenty-four . . . minutes ago you were in the bar downstairs and by yourself and ready to pick up anyone, anyone at all, ready to fuck anyone, because that's what you like. Twenty minutes ago you didn't know me and now you're showing me your tits, showing me *everything* – and I'm not even going to pay you, just fuck you. Keep touching it, put your finger in. *Put it inside.* Put your finger where I'm going.

You'd have done that in the bar, wouldn't you? Wouldn't you? You'd have sat on a table and lifted your skirt and fingered yourself so anyone could see you, any stranger, and that's why you're doing it for me. A total stranger and I'm going to fuck you. A total stranger fucking you and other strangers hearing it, hearing you get fucked, the whole thing. D'you want them to knock on the door later and fuck you, too? You do, don't you? You do. But I'm having you all for myself. And in the morning you won't know my name, you'll only know my cock . . . Oh, she likes that, that's got her. Roll over, all fours. Like a bitch. Come on. Come on. And I'll make sure they hear you. Come on. No, leave that, I'll do that. Lovely. Stay that way. Just like that and then you get my cock.'

'You're a bit tense.'
   'Not really.'
   'Only a bit.'
   'I didn't expect you to . . .'
   'What? You didn't expect me to fuck you? You were liking it all when we started and then −'
   'I did like it. I do. I just . . . We can do something else, we can −'
   'No, tell me how we make this work. Because you have a lovely − there it is − you have a lovely cunt . . . I thought that you'd . . . I thought it would be . . . Do you want me to put the light out?'
   'No.'
   'So you could concentrate.'
   'I *can* concentrate.'
   'Because you're wet. You're very . . . I mean, you were enjoying it and then you weren't.'
   'That's not true.'
   'You seem a bit tense, that's all. You know, why don't you decide what's next. All right, love? '
   'Are you annoyed?'

'No. And please stop asking that. I'm very pleased to be with you and I'm having a good time. But I can go away if you want. And I didn't intend to freak you out or anything. It was just playing.'

'I don't irritate you?'

'Darling, you're just bringing yourself – so much worry in one head – it's not that kind of night, is it? Not a heavy night and we've got to obsess about stuff together, eh? Bloody hell, love . . .'

'I'll suck you.'

'You're very kind.'

'I said I'd suck you. So I will . . . Now what? What's the matter?'

'But it's not a duty, love. Hey, why are you . . . ? Don't turn your head. I can't kiss you if you do that.'

'Why do you want to keep making this romantic, it's not romantic, it's . . . why call me *love*? And if you kiss me – you'll taste of . . .'

'I'll taste of you. Of course. I taste very much of you. I would. I've just spent at least ten minutes trying to get you to come – with my mouth.'

'Sorry.'

'I'm not complaining. Shit, I *am* complaining – you don't want it romantic, you don't want it horny . . . Could you be clear at *some* point and let me know how I'm meant to be here. For you.'

'I wanted to . . . I want to . . . I'm a bit confused.'

'You're telling me, love. Ah, there you go, though – a fucking smile. Haven't seen that for a bit.'

'Well, and you're confused, too – I'm a bitch *and* I'm your sweetheart?'

'You're both. Which is exactly what I want and why I want to stay. And why I've given myself a knot in my larynx, or pulled something vital, anyway, eating you out like a hungry hound.'

'Like a hungry hound?'

'Yeah. *Like a hungry hound.*'

'Don't go, though. Sit back down.'

'No, I'm going to rinse my mouth. And that'll be better? If I taste of spearmint instead of cunt?'

'You don't have to do that.'

'I do if I want to kiss you. Jesus, you've even killed my hard-on, which isn't how I wanted to say that – don't get worried again – but it was on its way back and now it's undecided.'

'Then I'll sort that.'

'You don't have to.'

'I'll sort it.'

'Okay . . . Determined bitch . . . Determined sweetheart . . . And down she goes. Oh. Kay. Steady, though – no need to be . . . Let me lie down . . . No, let me stand up. I want to stand up and you can . . . that's it. If you . . . that's it . . . Oh, what a girl you are. What a girl. But you don't have to be so . . . There's no rush. Christ, unless you do *that*. Oh, darling. More like . . . Oh, that's the way. And look at me, look up. That is the way. Sweet lips. Good lips. You looking at me and. My. Cock. In. Your. Mouth. Saw you and I wanted to fuck your mouth. Wanted this. I did . . . Nod your head if you're going to swallow. No, don't smile, not now – naughty girl. D'you want a mouthful of come? Do you? Suck it. Suck it. Jesus, I fucking like fucking your fucking mouth.'

'How are you feeling, love?'

'Fine. Great. That was . . . that was great.'

'I love you.'

'Why say that? Honestly, though? Why make this something it's not? Not that you're not . . . a good man.'

'A *good* man? I dunno about that. Don't think a good man would have had at you in every possible manner and place – except that one. But you do kind of want it there, too . . . Admit it.'

'I . . . I thought *you* would. I tried to–'

'I did notice . . . suddenly your tongue's up my arse, that did catch my attention. *Isn't she the pleasant surprise*, I said to myself. And you liked my finger up there – return the favour – and it'll be a lot better with my cock. I won't hurt you.'

'I've never done that.'

'You've never done any of this, you said.'

'Which was true. I don't go round picking up strangers . . . just you. And you're . . .'

'I'm what?'

'A lovely . . . choice.'

'And, ladies and gentlemen – she gets romantic. Just about. But will she be romantic enough to do me the honour of letting me very softly and gently and passion-ately screw her the back door way.'

'That would be . . . I'd remember that, wouldn't I?'

'You could lie back any night and think – *that guy took my last virginity.* I would love to do that. And you'd love it . . . And over she goes, persuaded, and let me see . . . Like a natural . . .'

'Yeah.'

'You're trembling, though.'

'That's all right.'

'Is it good trembling.'

'Yeah, good trembling. Oh. That's . . . That's . . .'

'My thumb. Relax. *Relax.* And . . . one finger. Let it happen.'

'This is . . . I want this. I do want this. I want you to have this. You have to take everything.'

'Which is what I intend. Two fingers . . . that's a brave girl.'

'No, I'm a bitch. A bad bitch.'

'Of course you are. Of course you are. And this is your punishment. Are you ready? There you go, there you go. Relax, though. No, you'll have to relax. No. No, stop, love. There's a bit of blood. We'll need to stop. No, I can't do it if you're –'

'Please. I want it. I want –'

'You want to lie down and I'll hold you. Don't cry.'

'I'm sorry.'

'It's okay. Not the end of the world. I should be sorry. Didn't do it right.'

'I wanted it.'

'We'll maybe try again later.'

'My mother? She taught me lots of things. Like the being polite. Saying *I love you*.'

'When you don't mean it.'

'I know what I mean. Just now.'

'Well, *I* love *you* if it's just now.'

'There now, was that so hard . . .'

'And you loved your mother.'

'Certainly not like this, I didn't.'

'But I can hear it in your voice – you loved her . . . You can always trust a man who loved his mother.'

'Who told you that?'

'My dad.'

'Did he love his mother?'

'I think so.'

'Fair enough. You look sleepy.'

'I'm just . . . resting.'

'So since you're not sleepy and we only have tonight and you're feeling better . . .'

'I want you in me again. For a long time.'

'Demanding, aren't you?'

'If we only have tonight.'

'No argument from me. So which would you prefer – a cherry-flavoured fuck. Or pina colada. You couldn't make it up . . . Or dealer's choice. A good, long, hard shagging and then tomorrow you'll still feel me, even when I'm gone.'

'If you do that I might want a repeat performance some time.'

'Greedy bitch. You never know. You never know your luck.'

'Are you married?'

'What?'

'Do you have a wife?'

'No.'

'Girlfriend?'

'No.'

'Anyone?'

'I have – do you really want to know? – I have a daughter who is fourteen and an ex and . . . not much else. Why? Do you want to tell me *you're* married? Is this *that* kind of thing?'

'No. I'm not. Married. No husband. No kids. No one.'

'I could put an ad in the paper for you – *Fantastic ride, up for anything, great lips, takes things a bit seriously, sucks cocks like a hooker.*'

'Charming.'

'I don't mean I think you *are* a hooker . . . You're a nice person. Sweet. I like you.'

'Why do you say I take things seriously?'

'Well, my darlin', we've been at this for . . . hours. And you don't really let go, do you? And you haven't really come.'

'I came.'

'Not properly.'

'I came.'

'Oh, sweetheart . . . that, that *is* sad. You know?'

'I'm sad?'

'No, no, *no* – it's only . . . I worry about you – gets infectious, worry – and yours has rubbed off on me – mainly rubbed off right there. I worry you've never had a *real* come.'

'And you're the expert, are you?'

'There's coming to please someone else and there's coming to please yourself . . . and there's not even knowing who you are any more and being more with someone than you ever have been – just losing it. *That's* coming.'

'Like your ex-wife did?'

'Was that necessary?'

'No.'

'No, it wasn't. It's just if you're married for any length of time you have all different kinds of sex. And *you* need the great big huge kind. Everybody does. So if you'll let me, I'll try and . . . you know . . . no pressure.'

'But I'm lousy at coming. Lousy at sex?'

'Don't be so complicated. I want you to have a great time. I am.'

'Why, though? Why would you want that?'

'Who *cares* why? I just do.'

'Why?'

'Because why not.'

'Why?'

'Fine, fine . . . Okay . . . Honestly? I had a job interview today . . . Yesterday now. Important. Life-changing important – the sort of stuff I never thought I'd get a chance at and I prepared and prepared and I put the suit on – best suit – and I drove down here and I looked at the town and I'm willing to relocate – I'm willing to commit, if they'll commit – and I did well in the interview, I genuinely believe they were impressed and I have a chance – I'm not sure, you can't be certain and I'm not going to get . . . excited – but I think . . . I do think that I did myself justice. They're going to call me on Monday, they said – at least that's not too long to wait . . . And I felt pretty good this evening – yesterday evening – and I came back to the hotel and I was *buzzing*, I was *alive* – the first time for I don't want to count: a decade:

more: since way before the divorce – I was so much alive that I didn't want to just go out and eat my dinner and then go up to my room. I wanted to talk, I wanted to be with people and I went to the bar in the basement and I didn't fancy it much, so I came up and tried the one by reception which was such a good move, so sweet, because there you were – you – alone – in the bar, too. This fantastic –'

'Woman with a mouth you wanted to fuck.'

'Don't make it like that. You were beautiful and sexy and on the surface you looked in control, but underneath it seemed, it was kind of there, that you'd do more than that – the way you walk – and you didn't ignore me – you wanted to talk to me, you wanted to be with me and flirt with me a tiny bit like a horny bitch – which we know you are – stop pretending you're offended and listen to how beautiful you are and important – and it was all fine – because it was like I was changing into the man they'd hire, the man who'd get the job, the man you'd go upstairs with. They knew in the bar. They saw me – who I could be. They knew I was going to – *we* were going to . . . fuck – make love, fuck, get each other happy. Those guys from Manchester, the loud wankers in the corner – one of them stared right at me as you and I walked out and I know he was jealous, because I had you – and he believed I was who I want to be – someone who makes it, man with a plan, someone who gets what he wants – deserves it – someone you'd come for.'

'That's not fair. I did.'

'Not enough.'

'Then I will.'

'Promise?'

'Yes. Promise. I like you. You're . . . you're beautiful, too. And I haven't got any idea why I went in there – into the bar. I don't like rooms full of strangers, but you, then you came in and looked . . . I thought I'd be able to talk to you – and you've got . . . your hair's great.'

'My *hair*?'

'You *listened* to me.'

'That's easy enough done – you don't say a lot.'

'I get . . . I'll say I'm so happy you're here.'

'And why is that? What is it you like about me? Tell me. What have I got here that does it for you?'

'Your . . . the way you touch me and your mouth and . . . your stomach is . . . and where your hair starts.'

'Oh, *that* hair . . . and what about my cock.'

'I love your cock.'

'Say that again.'

'I love your cock. It's beautiful and . . . so . . . It's the smoothest thing I've ever kissed . . . it's more . . . if they'd wanted to invent something, something wonderful that I'd need to touch and I love sucking it and having it in me and feeling it be itself in me.'

'Once you get going you're quite the talker, aren't you?'

'It's got a way of being. I'd know it now. If I ever . . . And I'm . . . I don't really believe we met, I can't . . . that something this good . . . I'll remember your cock. I'll . . . It's not really that I'll miss . . .'

'Oh, now, don't.'

'Sorry. Again.'

'Don't cry. Don't do that. No. Come here, love. No, come here. If you're going to cry you might as well do it here. That's it. Why don't you . . . take your mind off . . . whatever's . . . wrong. There's nothing really wrong. It's just us here and all the jealous bastards listening . . . God, I really don't know what to do here . . . Why don't you, why don't you kiss it some more. Yeah, that'll cheer you up. Sweet girl, you kiss it – I want you to. That's better. Isn't it. You do that for a while and keep it safe in your hand – yes, lovely – and you do whatever you want and I'll just lie back here and . . . let you.'

'Yeah, I miss my daughter. I still get to see her, but it's not much use. She thinks I'm a tosser.'
   'She'll grow out of it.'
   'Yeah? Dunno if I will. And moving down here won't help.'
   'She'd maybe stay with you for longer – make special trips instead of doing weekends and evenings and . . . it might be good.'
   'Stay with me? Yeah. Stay sitting in the house, texting her friends, being bored, ignoring me, refusing to eat. God. I'm not the best father, but *fuck*. I never did anything but the best for her. Nothing was my fault in the divorce. I haven't ruined her life. She's doing that all by herself.'
   'It'll work out.'
   'Yeah? Anyway. Enough of that. How about you?'
   'I'm okay.'
   'I didn't want to upset you. I didn't know.'
   'Well, how would you know? I'd taken off the sign from round my neck – *Mum's just died. In a mess.*'
   'Shhh. You're not in a mess. You're hurt. It's natural.'
   'There's nothing about me that isn't a mess.'
   'Trust me – that's not true. See . . . ? Not true. I'm going to kiss all the bits of you that aren't a mess. Okay? Okay?'
   'That's . . .'
   'And if it makes you cry again, that's okay, too. I'd even like it.'

'I had the same thing happen a couple of years ago – my mother – pneumonia. They gave her the wrong antibiotics and she died. It's crap. Makes you crazy. Makes you divorced, in fact.'
   'If it weren't for the funeral I wouldn't have said yes.'

'Oh, well. That's me told.'

'No, listen – I would have wanted to say yes, but I wouldn't have. Because I don't take chances. I don't . . . try things when I should. Since I was a kid – the same. Every time. Sitting against the wall at school dances, getting too pissed at parties, because then I won't mind when I go home and I won't keep going through the way I screwed up again. If I hadn't decided – *fuck it, my mother's dead, not me. There's nothing she can say, she can't stop me, thinking about her can't stop me – so, fuck it – I'm doing what I have to for once.* Any other time, I'd have come up here by myself and wondered what you would have been like – the cute guy in the bar. I wouldn't have found out. It's . . . yesterday was the shittest day of my life. Cremation. No one but me dealing with it. My dad died years ago and so I'm left choosing a coffin, for Christ's sake. A coffin. Does anybody think they'll end up doing that, ever? Genuinely? I had to decide what they'd burn, what her pals in their hats would see rolling back behind the curtains before they asked about my life and I couldn't give them answers – not one. Then after all that, I get an urn. And urn full of her. Mostly her – there's bits of other people, too, though, I saw a documentary and it was pretty clear, you don't know who you end with, really   A fucking urn. And when everyone's gone and stopped doing their duty, stopped being sorry for you – then you end up . . . so small – bloody tiny – bloody ugly.'

'You're not ugly.'

'Thanks.'

'Don't cry.'

'I'm not.'

'Just . . . kiss me. No, I enjoyed the talking, but let me kiss you. Let me. Let me fuck you – while you're . . . while you're soft. You're so opened up just now, you know that? It's beautiful. Soft. So we should fuck. We should go nuts, we should go crazy. Let it happen.'

'I can't.'

'Yes, you can. Let me. Just let me. And I promise you'll come. You'll come like you never have. My present. Let me. You want to. You do want to. No point shaking your head. Let me. Let me do it all. That's it, love. That's it. You take it. Let me. Let me. And then you'll cry. Then you'll fucking cry.'

'Sorry.'

'Nothing to be sorry about, love. I wanted you to . . . have a nice time, that's all.'

'You didn't upset me – I'm already upset. My mother died. That means you get upset – means *I* get upset. Sorry. I have to get used to it. The way I am . . . It's not your fault.'

'It feels like my fault.'

'It's not. You've been – You've helped.'

'That was a lot of crying . . . They'll have heard you next door.'

'They'll have heard us next door all night.'

'Up and down the corridor I would think. Dirty fuckers. Every word, every everything. I bet they made up pictures to go with it. I bet they'll stare at you over breakfast.'

'We might have annoyed them.'

'Then they could have gone away, stopped paying attention, stuck their fingers in their ears . . . People only do the things they want to – if they're honest, they know that – but then if they feel bad about them they blame somebody else. Unless they're like you – then they blame themselves.'

'I'm not blaming myself . . . But it was all right, though? Was I all right?'

'Silly monkey. 'Course you were. You were . . . the best present I've ever opened.'

'Well, since you'd seen everything else . . . why not see me falling apart. Would you have breakfast with me? Would that be okay? We could sit together.'

'You weren't falling apart – you were just coming and crying and crying and coming. You were amazing . . . I could ride you all my life. And look at the state of you. Sweetheart . . .'

'Yes. I must be a sight.'

'You're like a different woman – this incredible, wet, sweaty, sexy . . . I can see everything that's happened, I can see everything you've done – we've done – you're covered in it. You're amazing.'

'You said that.'

'Astonishing. You should know that.'

'Well. If you ever want –'

'*Shit!* Do you know what time it is? *Fuck!*'

'Shhh. No, I don't.'

'The curtain's all light, it must be . . . Where's my bloody watch . . . ?'

'It's here if you really –'

'*Shit.* It's five thirty. Five thirty tomorrow.'

'Really?'

'Five thirty-three precisely. I've got to drive home this morning. Fuck. When did we come up here?'

'About eleven.'

'*Fuck.*'

'But you've got time to . . . five thirty's still early. We've got time to, arrange things. Like . . . if you did want to know my name and I wanted –'

'*Fuck.* Sorry, what were you saying, love? I'm trying to work out which route in my head. If I can clear out of town before the rush hour . . .'

'I don't want to be needy.'

'Needy? Oh no, love – you're the least needy person I've ever met. Truly.'

'Now we've come this far, though . . . it might be . . .'

'I know. It might . . . Need to get my things together . . . God, but here are those tits . . . love kissing those tits . . .'

'Thanks.'

'Don't mention it. Hold that thought while I . . . My shirt smells of you. I think everything does, actually . . . Are you checking out today?'

'No. I have to go through the house: her belongings, clothes, ornaments . . . it'll take a while. She had a lot – not enough for a whole life when you think about it, but a lot – saved things – my toys, for God's sake. I found a box full of them yesterday. No end to the rubbish. And I can't seem to sort through it quickly – and I can't spend the night – not at her place, it's too . . . so I'll be staying here. I'll stay for the weekend. Until Monday.'

'Poor sweetheart. Where did you put my tie?'

'Over there. I'm not looking forward to it. In fact, I'm scared.'

'I bet. And I wish I wasn't rushing, but . . . Throw the covers back.'

'I don't know if –'

'You worry too much, I've said. Throw back the covers for me, love. Don't you want to give me a good send-off?'

'I don't want you to go yet. I mean, I know you have to. But this is still early, isn't it?'

'I said I'd be back by lunchtime.'

'Sure. I realise that.'

'Now get that sheet all the way off . . . and you can think of me tonight thinking of you. Ah, there she is . . . Are you a bit sore? Because of me?'

'Yes. I am.'

'Which is what you wanted, remember? Then when I'm out of here, you'll still feel me – in lots of places.'

'This is a bit quick. Isn't it? Quick?'

'I know and I'm so sorry. Let me do this a little bit, to make up for it – and this . . . you more cheerful now?

And – sorry, got to stop again – my jacket's . . . over your blouse. And there's my socks. And my shoes. And back to my sweetheart and you should put that away before I get . . . hypnotised and have to climb aboard again.'

'I'll stay like this.'

'That's my girl. Horny bitch. Well, you make that the last thing I see and then tuck yourself in once I'm gone and get some rest.'

'I'll be fine.'

'Yes, you'll be fine. You'll be totally fine . . . Oh, fuck it, let's have a cuddle. Here we go. Here we go . . .'

'I liked you.'

'And I liked you . . . And you're the longest I've ever fucked anyone – not my wife, not anyone – the whole of a night. Bloody hours . . . And you were gorgeous and you were sweet and you let me screw your arse.'

'Almost.'

'And that's as close as I've got. I'd only ever seen it in porn films before. And you let me. I'll never forget you were the one who let me.'

'That's . . . Good.'

'I am so sorry I have to run.'

'I'll be here. Until the weekend. During the weekend.'

'Which is a wonderful idea and I'd love to help you through your . . . trouble . . . and I'd love to get into this bed again and get into you again. Today. I mean, I could pull a sickie . . .'

'Could you?'

'No. God, no – I was away all yesterday, they'd never believe it. And I haven't got the new job yet. Stupid of me to suggest it, sweetheart. Very stupid.'

'No, it's okay. I understand.'

'Then I've got my daughter over on the Friday night and all of Saturday and . . .'

'It's okay.'

'I have the hotel number.'

'Yes, you would.'

'And I know your room number . . . Smile, love. It might never happen . . . As soon as I get a chance, I'll call.'

'You'll call?'

'That's right, I'll call. Absolutely.'

'You'll absolutely call.'

'I will. I will. I really will try. Okay, love?'

'Yes. That's okay. Of course.'

ANOTHER

They'd considered the child and kept themselves circumspect. For her sake they had been in love, but quietly. Angela had lost a father, she was only eight, she would need stability and to feel herself the centre of attention for a while. Lynne had been clear about this from the start – her daughter should be allowed time to adjust.

Jesus, they all of them had to adjust.

Barry Westcott, much-loved entertainer, goes to work one evening and then doesn't bring himself home. Vein burst in his head – vein, or an artery, his widow often cannot think of which – and out he goes. Found in his car. Key in the ignition, but he'd managed no further than that, which was a kind of miracle, or at the very least, a good thing – Lynne didn't want to imagine what damage he might have done if he'd started driving.

He'd made a remarkably natural-looking corpse. Natural for being dead. This meant he'd developed a bad colour – bluish-grey – mainly, though, he'd seemed puzzled and as if death had interrupted when he'd been just about to speak. The important thing was, there had been no injuries, or chains of subsequent accident and this could definitely be taken as having turned out for the best. Now people could think well of him, could let themselves enjoy unspoiled regret on his behalf, as they might like to. The press reports were kind and helpful, if rather small: 'Creator and voice of Uncle Shaun dies at 42. Widow speaks of fresh horizons tragically closed.'

This being how Lynne moved from *Barry Westcott's wife* to *Barry Westcott's widow* – not even the tiniest interval left between the two for independent life. And the transition accomplished entirely without her assistance. She never felt a thing.

Angela – perhaps permanently *Barry Westcott's daughter* – had, of course, been up and about the following morning with everything seeming usual and keeping quiet in case she woke her tired and grumpy actor dad and clearly supposing that she would see him when she came in again from school, oblivious to the phone calls and rushing and uniforms on the doorstep of the night before.

Angela has usually slept deeply and well. She lost the trick of it a little in the months right after, but it's back at the moment, she's mending. She has also forgiven, or chooses not to mention, that Lynne let her leave the house on that first Barryless day and spend so many hours unknowing, ungrieving, before the sadness was explained to her after dinner, her loss. It had been on the local news by lunchtime – then a slight delay and more national attention. That delay, it wouldn't have pleased Baz. Had he been still alive, ratty calls to the PR – Nina? Tina? – would have ensued: escalating complaints every twenty minutes until matters were resolved to his satisfaction. But, as Lynne had repeated to herself quite forcibly, this was the point of the coverage in the first place – Barry Westcott wasn't still alive.

It had struck her as peculiar that the announcement had seemed definitive when it was coming from a slightly tarty redhead in a studio and yet she hadn't found herself remotely credible when she'd tried to lay things out for Angela. The available information had not seemed realistic and somewhere in Lynne there had been a distracting certainty that she was inappropriately uninvolved. To be frank, it had been the sensible, the *loving*, choice to let a regional broadcaster summarise the changes in their household with an appropriate solemnity and some nice archive clips: Barry at a children's hospice, Barry standing in a line-up of dinner suits and shaking hands with Princess Michael, Barry in motion and then frozen as a permanently jovial and poignant close-up. Once she'd switched off the set, Lynne was surprised – not unpleasantly – by the start of her crying. The two remaining Westcotts had curled and snuggled with each other on the sofa for a while – *Barry's brave girls, united in heartbreak.*

Since their tragic and unexpected bereavement Angela and her mother – Lynne is also *the mother of Barry Westcott's child* – have settled into living somewhere delicate and withdrawn. They do not watch their television, because Angela no longer wants to, they have a number of extremely firm routines, are considering a kitten or a pup and they receive visitors who are markedly undemonstrative.

Primarily there has been one visitor who is called Richard. He is *your mum's pal.* When Angela is awake he only – and fairly infrequently – kisses Lynne on the cheek, or maybe squeezes her hand for a moment or says her name, 'Lynne,' – no more than that – and then, having caught her attention, he will let his eyes smile. His eyes are extraordinarily, professionally eloquent: the whites very white, the depths very deep. Lynne and Richard work hard to give no indication that *Angela's mother – Barry's widow* – is loved again.

Perhaps loved better than before.

Undoubtedly.

Undoubtedly loved better than at any other time before.

She would admit this, if anybody asked, and she knows that eventually they may ask: the large and curious *they* which is waiting outside in its hungry limbo, waiting to tell people who she is, who Richard is: papers, radio, magazines, television – so much telling.

At present, she and the girl are still insulated – *just living as normal a life as possible* – Lynne is proud of the neat protection she has built up for them both. And behind their little walls they do enjoy themselves. There have been trips when mother and daughter could share being puzzled by monstrous constructions in Lego bricks, or slightly unnerved by fancy-dress horsemen who plunged solemnly across the grounds of several castles and a stately home – each property filled with significant information and portraits of the neither recently nor disturbingly deceased. Or once there was that place where a man sold them honey and candles and furniture wax and showed off by spreading his face with a beard of bees. Angela and her mother have agreed that he was not educational, only mad. A lot of mad.

Having provided, with Richard's help, a number of increasingly successful excursions, Lynne has found herself looking forward to more, identifying a definite rise of excitement before packing up the car with drinks and *Just William* CDs and carrot sticks and hand wipes and setting the satnav to somewhere she has never been. When she giggles and runs across lawns holding Angela's hand, or waits in ice-cream queues, she no longer hears an interior voice attempting to undermine her – *this isn't you, this is sad pretending, this is absurd.*

Sometimes – as is reasonable and could be expected – the pair of them have welcomed company, they have been Angela, Lynne and Richard, enjoying treats. Richard happened to be around for Angela's particularly lavish eighth birthday party, the one intended to make up for the blank and hurt the year before. He played his guitar and sang for a while, performing with more authority than a normal, casual person should, but the kids all liked it because he was self-effacing, too, which was a difficult balance to strike, Lynne had thought. She had watched him and decided that. She had been impressed.

Richard had also appeared some evenings to talk about work, about the series, and to maybe stay for dinner. Eventually, he started to provide the bedtime story, oversee tooth brushing, get a kiss on the cheek before he stood up from perching on Angela's bed and turned out the light. He would never be there in the morning, though, would never give the impression he had spent his night mostly in Lynne's bed – *formerly Barry Westcott's bed* – running himself into hard hours, fierce and jerking hours, that pelted in after days of murmuring and politeness and knowing exactly, planning exactly, how they would end up. Not that they really kept to any plans – it was just ridiculously wonderful to make them, talk about them, consider possibilities.

And then at breakfast there would be no observable suggestion of the way they would hunt each other down to the bone in a tight, wet, beautiful agreement, or of his mouth so very open above her. Lynne was perfectly satisfied that Angela could eat her cereal with the lovely sliced banana on top after a sound and innocent sleep – Lynne and Richard were careful not to bang about or shout – and the mother could stand and watch the daughter and silently feel remade with good little private bruises, with resurrected skin.

'Is Richard coming today?'

'I don't know, love.'

'I like it when he reads to me.'

'Do you?'

'Does he read to *you*?'

'No, he doesn't read to me. That's special for you.'

'We're at the part where the snow's all melting and the witch can't go to anywhere because her sleigh gets stuck and she's immensely irritated.'

'Immensely irritated?' Lynne unable to resist stroking

Angela's shoulder at this – another example – which she will talk about to Richard – of how her offspring grows every day slightly more into a remarkably fine person – this happening with no apparent help from anywhere, more a slow uncovering of inherent qualities than anything learned or dictated. 'Is that right?' Another kind of miracle. 'Well, an *immensely irritated* witch would be a problem.'

'Richard says he's never read it before and I don't want him to miss it. Could you phone him and ask? If he'll come?'

'I'll phone in a while. I think he'll be sleeping now.'

'He'll still be in bed?'

'Yes. He'll probably still be in bed.'

'In his pyjamas?'

These unpredictable moments when she loved her daughter to the point of pain, 'That would be a silly place to have a bed – in his pyjamas . . . You'll have to ask him yourself if he wears pyjamas. He might have a nightgown instead, or a suit of armour.'

'But when you phone him you will order him to come here. If he's not busy with other people.'

Other people is pronounced with mild but unmistakable disapproval. It refers to everyone but Angela and Lynne. And Richard.

'Order him?'

'Yes.'

'We can't order him, he's a friend.'

'Oh –'

'But I'll ask. Now finish your cereal before it goes to mush.'

'It's mush now. I like mush.'

Which was the first Lynne had heard of this. Maybe the preference was recent. People did change, after all – if they were lucky.

Lynne had been lucky.

Eventually.

Recently.

She had finally found her luck.

In the beginning, Lynne and Richard were solely connected by business concerns. To be ruthlessly truthful, they never would have met without Barry – or rather, without Barry's lack.

Barry had died at an inconvenient time, professionally speaking. No one mentioned this in so many words, but it was there in the condolence calls from the various offices, which didn't fade and leave her be, but simply changed over the weeks into small remarks about Uncle Shaun having suddenly made a breakthrough: the books were really selling and so were the tapes, listening figures were great for the radio version and it would be another tragic waste – a minute one, but significant nonetheless – if they didn't somehow try to continue the brand's momentum. There was still serious enthusiasm for a television pilot, they didn't want to let that go: new series, new format, new medium – they were considering possibilities.

Barry hadn't wanted TV exposure, not as Uncle Shaun. In his opinion the audio versions were bad enough. By the end of Shaun's first year, Baz had been loudly and repeatedly *tired of doing kids' stuff*. But Uncle Shaun paid for the house, for Angela's schooling, for the green vintage Aston Martin from which paramedics would ultimately lever his body, so Barry persevered. He also made repeated efforts to catch the right kind of famous – he'd been playing in *The Caretaker* when he died, reminding the public of his full capacity. Respectable reviews.

This meant Barry would have found it amusing that without him there might be no more Uncle Shaun. However much he'd hated the character Barry had kept it close. He'd started writing the stories for Angela when she was three or four, maybe older – this was another set of details Lynne could not reliably recall. Barry had polished his versions and sent them out for publication when there'd been no money coming in, not even from voice-overs, not even from those bloody awful eye-drop ads. It was the first and only occasion when one of his bouts of creative despair bore fruit. The books were accepted and prospered. The audio versions had come along when they needed a replacement boiler and Barry had, despite himself, furnished a voice for *the nation's favourite uncle*. He had, indeed, been every voice: Bill Badger, the Llamas, Mr Pearlyclaws, everyone. Another demonstration of capacity.

But he wouldn't do telly.

With Barry, there was Shaun, but no telly.

Without Barry – no Shaun, but telly not a problem.

Being dispassionate, then: all that was needed would be another Shaun.

No one absolutely said this out loud – it simply became apparent, rose to the surface of every Shaun-related conversation and floated. Lynne pictured it bobbing and drifting, maybe slightly like her daughter's goldfish when it died.

Pets are always a serious undertaking, prone to calamities which may precede the recapitulation of older griefs – that's why the puppy and kitten options were still undecided. Richard was in favour, Lynne was unsure.

Lynne – *dead Uncle Shaun's widow* – did not express an opinion on the search for some fresh, theoretical Shaun and she didn't observe the auditions, because she'd assumed that would have been grotesque. She chose to be aware that they were taking place and to acknowledge that financial security was important, especially in unstable times. She was responsible for Angela's future. Lynne had, naturally, been a performer herself in her twenties, but she had no illusions about her talents and even the finest actresses could find middle age a hurdle:

not cute and young, not cute and old: you were grown up, that was all – and nobody wants that. Uncle Shaun would have to provide.

The production company sent her Shaun hopefuls on cassettes, to which she didn't listen. They also sent her DVDs, at which she didn't look. And then, for a while, there were more calls and a few letters, which mentioned how irreplaceable Barry might perhaps turn out to be. Lynne felt she agreed with this, should almost tell them – *yes, Barry was Barry and no one else*. Barry with the fake face for parties, Barry who loved to flirt, Barry who was scared, who was utterly terrified, that having a child would mean he couldn't leave Lynne if he wanted, couldn't upgrade, couldn't be comfortable with moving on. She'd understood this immediately in the hospital, in their first post-natal, post-paternal encounter. Barry Westcott, he was one of a kind.

A kind she'd been supposed to like. If you could no longer love, she had reasoned, you should try to like. Curiously, liking had been much more difficult to achieve.

Barry had offered her a child as a consolation for *his* inability to love *her*. (Liking was also beyond him.) In order to shore up something that couldn't stand, they had made a person: a complete, living human being. Reckless addition, that – no idea what they'd both been thinking – if they had, in fact, been thinking.

Although, Lynne *had* been thinking: otherwise, she wouldn't have stared at her husband as he first picked up his daughter, hefted her tenderly, gracefully, feelingly – so the nurses could not help but remember the scene, believe it – and she had thought – *Got you*. She'd seen his eyes: the wide, unfamiliar chill that was settling in them and she had thought – *Got you. Fuck you. Deal with that.*

It had surprised her – that she would allow someone else to exist simply to defeat her husband. Then she forgot about it. When you come across something this unusual, this far out of your character, you're best to forget.

Anyway, it was no longer true and therefore didn't matter.

And eventually Shaun might not matter, not to anyone but her – that's how it had seemed. The messages of irreplaceability became more insistent, apologetic, and then dropped away entirely. Lynne had assumed that the multimedia hopes for her husband's other creation were being laid aside. There would, no doubt, be efforts to exploit what material there was, but in the absence of further storylines, of the voice, of the man himself, then everyone's options were severely limited.

Until that final package had arrived.

When she picked it up off the hall floor, honest to God, it weighed oddly, gave an impression of internal mobility, like holding on to something when it flinches, blinks. The usual company label was there on the usual type of padded envelope and the usual cheap plastic boxes were inside holding the discs – audio and video recordings.

The slip enclosed read – *We really think he's it. Our Shaun. We would be so delighted if you agree.*

Richard was on the discs.

Richard Norland.

First time she'd seen the name.

He'd done other work, but she'd missed it.

She'd missed him.

Her intention had been to do some ironing, dissipate the tension that had apparently started cluttering the edges of every room – and this would allow her to hear the thing without feeling too uncovered, too close.

Except that didn't work.

Not remotely.

Because she'd pressed play and heard her husband's voices, his exact voices, reproduced – those silly, for-children voices, only they were better – there was somebody inside them, running about inside them and finding unexplored lights and fresh corners and a joy they'd never had, never delivered.

Made her cry.

Made her happy.

Didn't make her miss Barry.

Sitting down – couldn't remember dropping to a chair, but she must have done – sitting down and hearing a type of unnecessary beauty being threaded into something of her past – the iron, meanwhile, ignored and tinging, breathing steam – not a chance of her doing anything but listening until the talking stopped.

That was 'Uncle Shaun and the Living Fish Tree', read by Richard Norland.

His own words those, his personal sound, with the tone of a bedtime story, the idea of lips that were close, next to your ear. Soft as trust. Fearful as trust.

Not that you'd trust some actor you don't know who's good at impersonating a total bastard.

This a sensible time to grab up the iron and harry some pillowcases flat, move on to the sheets. She'd laughed at herself then, for being idiotic, trying to work up a crush based on the speech patterns of a ghost.

Still, the guy was good, you had to admit it – ideal. He'd avoided those sharp little inflections that used to signal how disgusted her husband was by the burden of entertaining children. Mr Norland had greatly improved upon that.

She'd waited another day to watch the DVD, partly in case it disappointed – but mainly because she was sure it would not and then where would she be?

Somewhere silly and hormonal.

A response to bereavement.

Or else somewhere I have never been and might like to go – no preparations, no map.

Because why not?

For once, why not?

There being no reason why not that she could find, she spent the following afternoon with her computer in a dimmer and dimmer living room as the day surrendered into a pewter sheen and then left her and she watched a man plainly demonstrate that being alive was something not everyone did well, or even adequately. On the DVD Richard Norland was working without working – something she'd never been able to do, that Barry had never been able to do – Richard had the knack of visibly racing to meet with the best of himself: no caution, no reserve, no need to please – he made himself an indisputable fact.

Lynne had wondered if there was such a thing as a beautiful fact.

She played the DVD a number of times.

Once Angela had eaten, done her homework, gone to bed, Lynne had emailed a response to the producers. She assured them, in general terms, that she was pleased Shaun seemed to be in such good hands. She suggested that, should Mr Norland wish, they might get together, discuss things. There would be matters to discuss.

There were days when this seemed insane.

There were days when she was certain this *was* insane.

There were no days when she wasn't going to attempt it – seeing him.

If he wanted to see her.

Which, it turned out, he did.

He sent an email. Formal. Polite. Anachronistically polite.

Perhaps he was pompous, pretended to be intellectual, was an arse.

No harm done if it fell flat, which it was likely to.

But you have to try.

She checked his CV a few days before they were due

to meet – in case they had something in common she should know about – or to feed the necessary small talk – or to check if he might be likely to be an arse – or to work out that at certain times he was ten years younger than her and at others only nine. A single-figure difference was okay.

Not that she'd been projecting.

She'd been pretending, playing. That was permissible, natural.

Telling myself a bedtime story. Nobody else here to do it.

She'd invited him up to her house. This made sense was logical. She would feel secure in her own home – previously *Barry Westcott's ranch-style country retreat* – and she'd asked Mr Norland to arrive at three thirty so that, should he turn out to be mostly illusory, no more than a bundle of skills, Angela would come in from school before the situation got too awkward and be reason enough to send him packing.

When Richard had appeared – five minutes early and with a pot plant held tight in big-knuckled hands – there was no trace of Barry when he spoke, but also not much of the softness she'd liked in the recording. He'd seemed nervous and was, as might have been hoped, smaller and quieter than he'd been in the audition. He'd worn an ugly brown pullover that she didn't see again and which gave the impression he was slightly thick around the middle.

Actually he is, but only very slightly.

Smoothed-looking face, rounded, with a heavy jaw and those clever eyes – measuring, judging, flickering about – then settling, studying. Lynne had, in their initial hour, a good many opportunities to study him back, because their conversation didn't flow. Eventually, they stared at each other. With no particular interest. Minutes passing limply. Lynne babbled for a while about Barry's career, of all things, and noticed she was inserting the word *obviously* into virtually every sentence.

They peered at each other some more.

They stopped drinking their cold tea.

Angela saved them. Her additional presence edged Richard into grinning, then joking, then talking to the mother through the daughter, to the daughter through the mother, letting everyone hide themselves enough to feel safe.

They decided they'd eat dinner together – might as well, there was enough for three – Lynne still calculated their food for three – and then it was Angela's bedtime and there was also the noise of Richard doing something – from the clatter, probably an unanticipated culinary something, which was slightly alarming – while Lynne was trapped upstairs in going through the evening drill and Angela complained about having to sleep when interesting events might be unfolding.

'It'll be boring. Grown-up stuff. Business. Yes, it will. Close the eyes and go to sleep, you've got gym tomorrow.'

Down in the kitchen, Richard had been busy. 'Hi.'

'I'd thought you were washing up.'

Two dishevelled mugs had been set on the work surface. He'd picked one up and held it out to her, left the handle free and let his fingers suffer the heat. 'No. I was making cocoa. And more washing-up.' There was a sense of him leaning forward in this and seeing what she would say.

'Great. I never can get enough washing-up.' She took the mug.

Richard flapped his hand to cool it and stared towards the window and its bluish dark. 'If you have any we could throw in a dash of brandy, or rum or something and be grown-ups. Or leave it alone and just be kids.'

'We'll leave it.'

'Okay.'

They'd wandered through with their childish drinks

and sat on the sofa in front of a television with a disconnected aerial.

'Why don't you sell it, then? Or give it to someone?'

Lynne hadn't answered. She'd been thinking – *he's nothing like a total bastard. That's a promising start.* She was already constructing the ways they might say goodnight. And then halting the construction. And then starting it up.

They parted that night – as she'd predicted several times – with a hug: an initial hesitation and then a firm, slow, unthreatening embrace. She'd realised they were both testing what it meant, prolonging the contact out of caution, rather than desire. There was a tiny change of pressures and emphasis as he said, 'Thanks. That was a great evening.'

'No trouble.'

'We didn't really talk that much about Shaun.'

'Some other time.'

He'd drawn back at this, held her shoulders with both palms. 'Okay. You're on. I'll write down some points we should cover and bring them with me.'

'That'll be fine.'

Their progress had been infinitesimally slow, partly because Richard had been dating someone else and only gradually sabotaging what was left of that relationship by obsessing about Shaun – how would he dress, what would be his best haircut, even making notes towards fresh plot lines. He was also spending regular evenings with Lynne – *Uncle Shaun finding a new lease on life.*

It had taken them nearly a year for Lynne to finally hear him as she'd intended, to lie with his breath against her neck and the hot surprise of word after word slipping into her arteries, her veins, she didn't mind which.

This being how Lynne became *Uncle Shaun's lover* for the first time.

Obviously, this was an arrangement that not every-body would understand. There might be questions that Lynne didn't feel like answering if their situation became public and so they delayed, kept themselves exclusively to themselves.

What we are is mine, is ours and no one else's.

And is what Angela needs.

The other evening Lynne had been passing her living room, the door open and Richard and Angela inside, intent.

'Do you want *The Magician's Nephew* or *The Silver Chair* – which do you think?'

'I don't mind. You pick.'

'This one, then.'

They'd been standing at the window, no lights on and the sunset beyond them, catching them with edges of light: one tallish shadow and one short.

'But could you say a bit of 'Love and the Moon' first? Like about a page of it? Now? Could you?'

Neither figure moved.

'You want me to do 'Uncle Shaun and Love and the Moon'? Really?'

'Yes. And if . . . with the way you say it.' The child touching Richard's arm, sliding her hand lower to hold his.

'Are you sure you want me to?'

'Yes.'

A fury of purple and yellow at the sky's foot and her daughter turning to look up at a face.

'"Badger Bill wasn't there. Uncle Shaun had been looking for him all day, but he still wasn't there."' A dead voice risen.

Lynne had moved on as gently as she could, so as not to interrupt them. She'd gone into the kitchen to make cocoa.

When she'd returned to Angela and Richard they'd

been sitting alongside each other, the girl's head resting against the man's chest as if she was about to sleep.

Lynne paused and watched them and made certain that she thought – *This is the way we were always meant to be.*

VANISH

It had been her fault, entirely. Dee's fault – the whole bloody evening.

Which, to be truthful, made him slightly glad – it was, after all, three months since she had hurt him a new way. Tonight, in her undoubted absence, she was letting Paul feel reconnected, touched.

He'd bought the tickets for her just before they'd split, intending to give her a treat – an almost-birthday treat – 19 October and a trip to the West End, a fairly pricey dinner first and then off to a show. 19 October meant pretending she was a late Libra instead of an early Scorpio – as if that mattered a toss and would in any way have made her not a car crash as a person. Paul didn't even read horoscopes, she was the one who read horoscopes, he thought they were total shit. Probably, if he checked somewhere, consulted a website, it would be set down as axiomatic that early Scorpios were also total shit. But at that point he'd been trying for her, he'd been keeping the faith and imagining she would come through and turn out to be – *What? Sane? Undamaged? Undamaging?* – he could no longer be bothered to guess.

For the usual reasons, he'd gone the extra mile again, got hold of tickets before the place sold out and reserved them two seats in their future, side by side and near the front without being too close, because that could get scary. This magician bloke was somebody she'd talked about – she'd said he was really good – and there was bugger all she thought was really good on anything like a consistent basis – himself included – and the guy was going to be in London for a limited engagement, which sounded exclusive, sounded right – so everything should have worked out fine.

Everything might have worked out fine.

She could have enjoyed it.

The chances of that happening had been quite high.

But then she'd done a runner, she'd ditched him, and this time it was clearly permanent.

And Dee hadn't even known about the tickets. This leaving a possibility that had swung away now and again from beneath Paul's feet: a trapdoor thought of her being in the theatre anyway: of their meeting in the foyer, on the stairs, in the stalls: his hope and fear interleaving, building up an uneven, uneasy stack.

I didn't see her, though. The whole evening I didn't see her. And I almost did look.

Frankly, I don't believe she'd have got it together enough to have come along. So why would I see her? How could I?

And I did look.

I did, in fact, very much look.

I stared so hard things went all cinematic – felt like I was the one who wasn't really here.

For a while, he'd assumed he would tear both the tickets up – or else ignore them until their relevance had faded.

And then, at the turn of the week, he'd decided he ought to enjoy the whole experience on his own, reclaim it. Naturally, he'd skip the dinner and the effort at romance. There wasn't another woman he could take – a substitute, stand-in, fresh start – it just so happened there was no one new to hand and that kind of thing would, in any case, only hurt him: he wasn't ready for it yet. Nevertheless, he'd been fully persuaded that he should set out for an evening of having fun.

Even if the chances of fun happening had been quite low.

He'd dressed nicely – best suit, a flashy tie which he'd regretted and had taken off almost at once – it was folded in his pocket now. For some reason he had forgotten that nothing made singleness worse than being well turned out. If he could look good – and he did look pretty good, pretty easily – then his being not on the arm of a lovely escort was down to some deeper problem, an internal flaw.

Kind eyes, decent haircut, reliable mouth – somebody said that once: reliable mouth – but repeatedly bolloxed relationships, year after year. Must be broken where it doesn't show, then – something important about me gone missing, or else never arrived.

Dee – she said that I had a reliable mouth. So that probably doesn't count as true.

The other sodding ticket hadn't helped him: a leftover left with a leftover man, it had been a problem at once, already heavy in his pocket as he'd walked from the Underground, wandered up and eyed the posters hung outside the theatre: high monochrome repetitions of the magician's face.

He does *have a reliable mouth.*

Jesus, though, I don't even know what that would mean, really. Reliable, unreliable . . .

He has a mouth, that's all. Right where you'd expect. There it is, under his nose and over his chin – a mouth.

And he looks like a twat.

At least I don't do that.

The rhyme had made him smile – something from the Dr Seuss version of his life.

My girl let me down flat.

She is also a twat.

Paul had fingered the ticket and known he couldn't sit beside cold air, a ghost.

Which was why he'd turned up slightly early – this way he'd have some time to make enquiries in the queue.

'Hi. I have a spare ticket – do you want it?'

Clearing his throat and then being more assertive: 'Would you like this?'

Or maybe less assertive: 'Excuse me, would you like this?'

He'd been asking people who didn't have tickets, who wanted tickets, wanted them enough to come down here and wait in the hope of returns and who should have been pleased by an opportunity like this, an act of uncompromised generosity.

'Hi. Oh, you're together – this would be no use then.' These ones had been bastards – a matching pair of self-satisfied bastards – covered with certainty, with the spring of the sex they were going to have tonight. 'No, I'll look for someone by themselves. I wouldn't want to break you up. I'm sorry.'

'Yes, it's a real ticket.'

'Good evening, I just wondered . . .' He'd noticed he was starting to sweat. 'I have an extra ticket. There's nothing wrong with it. It's for quite a good seat – look.' The bloody thing had warped where he'd been touching it too long. 'That's a good seat.'

People had acted as if he were offering them a snake which would always sound rude, now he thought about it, rude more than poisonous – *Hi, would you like my snake? I have this snake. Free snake. Free to a good home. Tired old snake seeks any deargodplease home that it can get.*

The best thing was truly, genuinely not to think of anything to do with sex at present. And maybe not ever again.

'Yes, you would be sitting next to me. Sorry.' Talking to women – had he, at any time, known how he should do that? 'Is that a problem? I'm not trying to . . . We'll forget about it, okay? . . . No, just forget about it. Really.'

That's how you end up with the crazies – by never learning how you ought to reach the normal ones. 'You don't have to pay – I've paid. Sorry, that was me being ironic.'

Not that I expect you to appreciate that, or to find it amusing – but trust me – trust my perhaps reliable mouth, which I am not moving in case it shows you how I think – trust me while I do think, quite loudly, that I am laughing with my brain.

Leastways, maybe not laughing, but there is definitely something going on with me and with my brain. I think it is, perhaps, packing in advance of being gone.

'No, I don't want any money. The ticket's just no use to me . . . Well, if you want to pay me – then the price is written on it. Forty-five quid . . . Yes, it *is* a lot, but then it *is* a good seat . . . Well, twenty quid isn't forty-five quid – that's like . . . that's like you're . . . I'd rather you didn't pay me. Either nothing or the price, how would that be . . . ? I'm finding it quite hard to understand why you don't opt for nothing . . . No, I wouldn't want to do that – it would hurt. *But feel free yourself.*'

He'd never been aware of it before, but he did fairly often grit his teeth.

Then again, he did fairly often have reason to.

'Ticket . . . ? Ticket?'

Eventually someone had tapped Paul on the shoulder – this causing the foyer to ripple, contract, until he'd realised he was looking into an unfamiliar manic smile. The person smiling was slightly goth-looking but clean, perhaps a student, had said his name was Simon and had asked if he could have the spare seat. Paul released the ticket with a kind of joy, or else at least a kind of satisfaction, because he was working on the principle that if you wanted something you should get it, you absolutely should, no matter who you were or how ridiculous your need. This was the only magic that might ever be worthwhile and should therefore be demonstrated, encouraged to spread and thrive.

Thus far it had only affected Simon, of course: granting him a seat he could not have afforded, even if he'd made it to the head of the returns queue. The excitement of this and his relative proximity to the stage, once they were both seated, made Simon chat a good deal, which Paul had not anticipated.

'This is beyond . . . this is out of this world, is what this is. I just couldn't get off work, only then I did, only *then* I hadn't got a ticket, but I thought I'd have a go in any case, and *then* the bus broke down – I mean, what would be the probability of *that* particular bus breaking down on the way to *this* particular theatre? I *had* to *run*. From *Regent's Street*.'

Paul tried to calculate the probability of *his* breaking down while seated in the stalls of *this* particular theatre.

Simon, it was clear, had an overlarge capacity for joy. 'He's amazing – The Great Man. They call him that – TGM. The initials. Did you know that? TGM. Not just us – his crew, his assistants, everyone *in the business*.'

It was ridiculous and unfair to imagine a person like Simon could unknowingly drain each remaining pleasure from those around him and leave them bereft. 'Do you know his work? Amazing guy. I've seen every show.' Even so, as Simon cast his hands about, shifted and stretched, Paul found himself taking great care that they didn't touch, didn't even brush shoulders, just to be sure that no draining could take place.

'The show before this? – *Mr Splitfoot*? – what a night. You see your first one and you always think he couldn't top it – but then he does. Excels himself. Over and over. *The lesson of excellence*. I had to go to Southport for him last January, can you *believe* it? *Southport*.'

Paul found he *could* believe in Southport but was primarily very happy to allow a new and gentle sliding thing to peel out across his mind and muffle him, make him almost sleepy, something close to sleepy: certainly opened, unsteady and soft. Simon was still talking – Paul could feel that – but the young man was also apparently dropping, further and further: falling with his sound beneath him into the wider and deeper, changeable din of individuals fitting themselves to an audience, becoming large, expecting. Their want teased and pressed at Paul's will and he tried to join them in it, to let go.

I don't know, though. I don't know.

The theatre was an old one: gilt and rose-painted mouldings, candle brackets and layered galleries, rattling seats of golden plush and a chandelier there above them, holding up a monstrous threat of light.

I don't know.

Paul could appreciate the beauty of it, obviously – only he'd caught this other sense as well: that every charm was closing on him, folding down into a box, a mechanism already carefully set and working. He could almost hear it tick: cogging round to make him overly substantial, dense. And the ushers – it had seemed there were too many ushers, too many men dressed in black with unusual shoes who paced and watched and loitered casually, stood by the stage and by the entrances, moved with a purpose that made them another part of the elaborate, obscure machinery, of a building that had turned into a game. Paul didn't much like games – they made him lose. He didn't much like anyone who played them.

But it's just a performance. It's magic: that kind of game. If I think something's going on, then it probably might be, but there's no need to fret. It's nothing personal – it's just the magic, not anything wrong.

All of these people, packed in snug: they'd sent the air up to a blood heat and he'd liked that, which surprised him. And maybe this was how the game would work him – making him trapped and then offering release: the hope of joining something strange, the chance to be lost in the mind of a crowd, to evaporate. It had been, in a way, extremely welcoming.

I don't know, though.

Straight ahead had been the tall, naked dark of the stage. It stared at him, prepared.

Everyone else in here understands this. They're going to like it. They want to play.

I might not.

Then his morning fear had tickled unexpectedly in his chest − the creep of it as he would get out of bed and be alone − no one else there, nobody's belongings, only time in the flat and books he didn't read and DVDs of films he never really fancied watching and maybe this would be the way it was from here on in − forever − maybe even with somebody there he was meant to love, trust, be loved by, maybe even then it would stay the same, had always been the same: himself locked some-where airless, somewhere dead.

This evening is all of the things that she would like. Not me.

And he'd sat inside this thing that Dee would like while panic tilted in his neck and signalled a chill to the small of his back. He'd begun to wish hard that the lights would go down before he cried.

And then they did.

Like magic they did.

At the perfect point.

Exactly when another moment's wait would have toppled him, the colours had mellowed, the auditorium was withdrawn, was dimmed to exit signs and its private variety of night.

Evaporate now and nobody would see.

Nobody would stop me.

Or nobody would help.

There was no music.

Just breath – the audience noticing its nerves, stirring, giggling, settling again and holding.

Paul had shut his eyes. He'd inhaled the vaguely sweet and powdery warmth, the taste of attention, of other lives.

All right, then.

He'd tried to concentrate, to push and lift away from the restrictions of his skin, his skull. He was very tired, he'd realised, and had a great desire to be peaceful, uncluttered, unharried – to be not himself.

All right, then.

He'd begun to hear footsteps and, for an instant, they had seemed so natural, so much the start of an answer to soften his current need, that they might have been some internal phenomenon, an oddly convincing idea. Then they grew sharper: the hard, clear snap of leather soles that paced, perhaps climbing closer – yes, there was definitely a suggestion of stone steps winding upwards to the stage and raising an authoritative, measured tread. The sound was just a touch peculiar, amplified, treated.

All right.

Paul had unfolded his arms.

Yes.

He had let his hands rest easy on his lap. He'd blinked.

Yes.

He'd looked clear out into nowhere, into the free and shapeless deep of everything.

Do what you like.

And Paul had grinned as the footfalls halted, the proper pause extended and then the magician had walked out from the wings.

You do just precisely whatever you would like.

And The Great Man had been – *What?*

Sane?

Undamaged?

207

Undamaging? —

'Oh, what did you think, though? Really. I *mean . . .*' When the final applause was done with, Simon had been not unexcited. 'First half – *fantastic*, but second half? Always a kicker.' He'd clutched at Paul's forearm, shaking it gently. 'What did you *think*? I didn't ask in the interval, I held back – didn't I hold back? – but *how* was *that*?' Simon had cornered him up at the top of the aisle, turning to peer back into the emptying theatre, the emptied stage. He'd pulled his free hand through his hair, smiling, then shaken his head and laughed. 'Jesus, how *was* that?'

Paul had smiled, too – although he'd also shrugged away from Simon's grip. Then he'd breathed in – tasted deep – tasted something like physics going quite awry, like unexpected possibility. 'It was all right.' He'd thought, for a second, the game might not be over.

'It was –' Simon had interrupted his outrage and checked Paul's face. 'Oh. Yeah.' He'd grinned. 'It was all right.' He'd seemed to consider for a moment. 'You feel a bit weird, yeah? Bit stunned? Mugged? Fuddled?'

To Paul, it hadn't felt quite appropriate that someone who was barely past teenage, who probably had at least one bad tattoo, and a no doubt exhaustive regimen of mildly unnerving self-abuse, was asking Paul about his personal condition.

Still, a response would do no harm, 'A little – a bit weird. Maybe. Yes. That stuff that he did with the . . . the dead . . .' It was sometimes good to make a conversation, join in.

'Then you should come along with me. You'll like this.' Simon had leaned in close enough to prove that his breath smelled of crisps. 'The show after the show.' But he'd also been unmistakably very serious and almost tender. 'Honest. It'll be good.' Simon had padded off without another glance, repeating as he went, 'How

was that . . . How just the bloody hell was that . . .
How *was* that . . .' He'd expected Paul to follow.

And Paul had.

*This isn't a chat-up, though, is it? Even if I was gay, he
wouldn't be my taste at all – embarrassed if he'd think he
was . . .*

*Then again, he's clearly a nutter – so probably I'd fall for
him completely.*

Walking out of the theatre and round the bend.

*Oh, quite exactly round the bend. And maybe here is where
I get mugged. Factually, unmagically mugged. He'd be a really
useless mugger, though – a lover, not a fighter: young Simon –
well, a wanker, not a fighter. But he could have pals – mugger
chums. Maybe.*

Around one more corner and they'd stopped in a little
lane.

*This exact and precise little lane – mildly cold and un-
mistakably damp and faintly piss-and-disinfectant-scented
lane – this lane at the back of the theatre where I am
currently standing. After all this time. Still standing.*

Worries had reeled by, but had left Paul curiously
sanguine – unworried, in fact.

Still am – calm as you'd like.

Simon had brought him to see the stage door and the
jovially restless cluster of other young men in black drain-
pipes, or disreputable coats, plus a scatter of slender,
underdressed girls and a few motherly types.

'He'll be out in a while,' Simon had murmured as if
he were in church. 'It's what he does. He comes and
speaks to us.'

Paul had been mainly glad he didn't have to go home
yet, but he couldn't help asking, '*What*? Who does?'

'TGM. It's what he does. No photographs, no auto-
graphs – says then it isn't friendly – but he'll chat. To
everyone. To you. Then it's like you're friends. We're his
friends.'

'You're kidding.'

'Why would I be kidding?' Simon had frowned, but then was interrupted by the appearance of two stocky pals – real, non-mugger pals – in what Paul thought must be second-hand suits – or they possibly both enjoyed wearing their dads' clothes. While Paul watched, the three men had shaken hands and fussed in each other's pockets, producing a flurry of small trophies: wallets and house keys, bus passes and condoms and christknewwhat, which they had passed between themselves for a while, deadpan – stealing and passing, returning, then stealing again.

After reclaiming his unlikely handkerchief for the third time, Simon had nodded to indicate Paul, 'This is Paul. He gave me a ticket.'

'You want to watch that.' The more solemn newcomer had tugged at his walrus moustache and extended his arm. 'Hi. My name's Mr Palm.' He winked. 'You can call me Morritt.'

'And I would be Knot. Not Not – and not Knott – a K and one T – Knot. Davenport Knot – it's a family name.' The unmoustachioed Knot waved politely and inclined towards Simon, 'How many did *you* sneak in? Any? Were you trying? Did you get any? A few? You did try? Was there the offer of a finger ring at any point? A bit of badinage and wordage?' He'd nudged Paul lightly, 'Beyond me to say how fine it is, splaying with words. Word splay. Words play well, don't they? Don't you just love words? Love-me things, love-ly things.' He'd grinned, over-broadly, and then snapped his whole face into neutral, examined his thumb.

Simon had shrugged at Paul, 'They're feeling antisocial. So they're being . . .'

'Playful.' Morritt had winked again, 'I'm always anti-social. Comes of being a sociopath.'

'Like I said, they're not in the mood for company, so I'll escort them and conduct what I will not at all or in any way describe as a debriefing over there.'

Morritt let his eyes grin but kept his face immobile and seemed to be searching Paul for something – not predatory, but curious, forensically interested.

'Morritt, leave him be.' Simon had patted Paul's shoulder, 'I'll be back in a bit. And –' He grinned like the boy he almost still was, 'Thanks again. Wouldn't have missed it.'

Which is how you end up standing by yourself and waiting. In a lane at night with your feet getting chilled – waiting for no one you'd wanted to meet in the company of strangers. And most of the strangers have headed off home.

All of the motherly women have gone, given up – except for the one with the shopping bag full of papers. Paul knew not to talk to *her* any more – and not to make eye contact, because that would start her off, as well.

'These are letters for TGM. I send them, but I know they don't get through. So I bring him the copies myself. He always smiles at me. He's lovely. He should eat more fruit.'

Paul had already been caught by her twice – once with the letter story and once with the much more complicated crap about there being some kind of grand conspiracy against magicians in general and TGM in particular – because he was so highly skilled – and only she knew how to stop it and TGM was fully aware of this and would one day ask her for her help which she would then graciously give. She was called Lucy.

Didn't want to know her name. Didn't want to know anything about her, or have anything to do with her. Funny, cos she's madder than anyone I've ever met and she does have nice tits. Big, anyway.

And she'd be grateful for the attention.

Sweet Jesus, what am I turning into?

And he glances at his watch to distract himself and it's ten past one and everybody's still here waiting – well, not so many as there were, but definitely some, a small crowd

– eight people, counting himself, which he does, because he's people – and Paul has no way of being sure if this is normal – a three-hour wait. He doesn't like to interrupt Simon and his friends to ask them, because they seem to be enjoying themselves, giggling and showing each other cards, coins, little gadgets, and if he steps into that and messes it up for them, then he'll be the boring old bastard who knows nothing and shouldn't be here and he's sure that will make him depressed, so he won't attempt it and then he thinks that maybe the magician is busy and – here it comes as quick as fainting, weakness, shame – the sly, worst possible thought comes ramming in – he imagines that maybe Dee *is* here, maybe she came, maybe she'd talked about the magician because she knew him and maybe they're in there now, in his dressing room – lots of lights and a countertop, mirrors and maybe – why not? – a bed – or a table – no, a bed – no, a hard, clinical table – and maybe he's touching her, maybe they're doing it, doing weird stuff, magician stuff, things that take three hours and counting, things that make her think the little bastard's really good, that open her and make her squeal it – he has this image of her skin and smears of make-up, stage make-up, of things that appear and disappear.

Except that's mad.

So mad it hurts.

Madder than Lucy.

I have no reasons to believe it, not a one.

Stark, staring Lucy.

Mental.

As stupid as staying here when I ought to just chuck it and head for home.

But I've been here so long that I might as well keep on.

Paul's vaguely nauseous, though – images of clever fingers and slippery skin pitching in at him, so he walks a bit, strolls round, swallows and rubs his eyes, as if this will make the brain behind them sensible.

In a doorway, one of the three remaining girls is sitting and holding a programme and Paul thinks the step beneath her must be dirty and that's not right and she'll be perished and, to distract himself, he goes over and suggests, 'You could have my jacket. Borrow my jacket.'

She has dull blonde hair, 'No, it's okay,' and tiny wrists which manage to make Paul feel she has sometimes considered slashing them.

'You look freezing.' He wants to hold her, finds he is talking as if they have met before, are friends – the way you talk to people when you know how to talk to people.

'No, it's okay.'

She doesn't seem annoyed by him or anything, so he sits down next to her, is quiet for a bit, gives her time, and then, 'Do you like him – the magician?'

'Yeah.'

'And you want him to sign that. Your programme.'

She tucks her feet in nearer to herself, to the backs of her thighs. This will wrinkle her skirt. 'I don't think he's coming to see us tonight. It's late. He wouldn't make us hang around this long. Something must have happened. Guests. Or he's tired. Everyone else has come outside. Not him. He's gone another way.'

Paul sees how she is curled all to the left, beside the wall: trying to keep cosy, and thinks this must be uncomfortable and ineffective. Her blouse is old-fashioned, Laura Ashley, something like that – he can't really tell in the shadow.

'TGM doesn't sign things.' She yawns just enough to put a tremor in her jaw: a sweet, sweet trembling.

'No. I forgot.'

'What did you think?'

'About what?'

'The show.' This makes her begin to smile and he can imagine the same gentle, drowsy expression being there for some person who cares about her, lighting for them in a dawn with pillows and the spread of her hair. She faces him – perhaps studying, perhaps amused, he can't be sure – and asks again, 'What did you think? You haven't been before, have you? Whatever funny little club we are, you're not really in it yet.'

Paul wants to yawn, to join her in that – because yawns are infectious and he is tired and it would be very easy for him to tremble, 'I thought . . .' offer her a piece of himself that might seem sweet, and he would – by the way – like to see her hair on a pillow, anyone's hair on his pillow, 'I thought . . .' But it's too late for that, doesn't matter, and it's fine for him to tell her now what's true – tell her as he would in a first morning when every- thing is interesting and you want to talk and you feel that you'll never get all that you need of this new woman and who she is and what she might enjoy and there is no pain from anywhere, not yet. 'I thought . . .' It's addi- tionally fine – it will be absolutely fine, any disclosure – because in the morning this blonde whose name he does not know and will not ask will have forgotten him entirely. He'll be gone. 'I thought he was great.' All gone.

'But?'

'No but.' He smiles to reassure. 'Really. There's no but.' He knows he can hold her hand and she will not take it amiss, so he does, squeezes her fingers, cuddles them, and they sit together in the doorway with the cold of the stone underneath them and he says, 'I thought he was very good at what he does and . . . it was how he did it. Because of him not being that big, you know? He didn't look like a big man, not tall – and not, not some twat in a campy suit, or a Gandalf beard, or some kind of . . . I mean he's not a twat – and he was like my size – and ordinary, average – smart but average – and trying so hard to make these things happen, these bonkers things – and they did – he tried hard enough so that they did. I mean, it wasn't easy. Not that I didn't think he'd manage, just that it wasn't easy. He had to fight. It's all just fake, I get that – but he had to *fight* – he took the trouble to make it seem beyond him, impossible – and then he beat it. He won.'

Paul begins again with, 'For people like me . . .' and then lets it fade. And he won't even attempt, 'And he was – he was like he was *magnificent* – because if you win you're allowed to be magnificent. You should be.' Because he thinks it would send him a little bit weepy – the way he'd got when there'd been that section in the second half: business that used a length of chain. He'd remember the chain: had a strong suspicion he would dream it, because it already had been half turned to a dream when it was presented, there had been a quality about it that had slipped right in.

'When it lifted, when the chain lifted . . . It's a trick, I know it's a trick – but it was right . . . It was the way that you need it to be.'

She squeezes *his* fingers now. 'Like something coming true.'

It is pleasantly, slightly painful to consider this. 'Yeah.' The word seems damp and fluttery in his throat.

'That's what I come for.' And she pecks his cheek. 'That's why I come. To see that. Because it isn't real anywhere else.' And then she lets him go, because they are nothing to each other, he is nothing to her. 'I think I'll head home now.'

He is nothing to anyone. 'Will you be all right?' His knuckles feeling unnerved, stripped. He has the hands of no one.

'Yes.'

She stands, slightly unsteadily and Paul rises with her and holds her shoulder for a breath. 'It was nice meeting you.'

'And it was nice meeting you.' This before she walks away, aiming for the street and a cab, he guesses. No other options beyond a cab at this time of night. Unless she's walking. Alone. Alone might not be safe.

Paul shouts after her, 'You'll be okay? Do you need somebody with you?' But she half turns, waves her programme at him and shakes her head, keeps on round the corner and back to the usual, old world.

The other girls must have given up too, when he was occupied elsewhere, so there is Paul now and there is Lucy and Simon and his two companions with their imaginary names – each of them staring at Paul because he has called out. 'Sorry!' Although he isn't sorry. Quite the reverse.

Simon ambles over, 'No, *I'm* sorry. This is *crazy*. He's *never* this late. It's . . . he never doesn't come out, but he never leaves it this late, so I don't know, mate. Don't think badly of him.'

'I don't.'

'Don't think badly of magic.'

'Oh, I don't.' Paul thinking of nothing but that chain: broad links, dull and heavy, dragged into the air, driven upwards by pure will and then compelled to disappear: a whole building of human beings casting them away and the magician there to hold their wish, find it, touch it out and show a proof of what they were and could be.

Just a trick. And just that last tangible moment before you're free – seeing that, for once seeing that. And if you can see it, then it can be and nothing left to hold you back. 'I don't think badly of it. Really. I had a good time. Thanks.'

Just a trick. But I could see it, see myself.

Now you see it.

Yes.

'You going home? It's past two.'

'Is it?' Paul's watch agreeing that suddenly it is past two and on the way to three. 'Oh. Might as well hang on a while longer, though – d'you think?'

Simon takes a pound coin and folds into his hand and out and back and melts it somewhere between his fingers. 'Yeah, might as well.' He shrugs. 'Come and join us, guys.' He beckons his friends. 'The smug one's Barry and the miserable one's Gareth – his mum's Welsh.'

Gareth wanders towards them, avoiding Lucy, 'She *wants* to be Welsh. That's different.' And Barry follows, nodding.

The four of them slouch together in a huddle – they shift and cough.

'When he *does* come out . . .' Gareth tugs his moustache.

Barry reaches round and tugs it, too, 'You mean *if.*'

'When he *does* come out, we should all just ignore him – like we're expecting someone else.'

They grin.

'No, but that would be rude, though.' Paul's sentence fading as he starts to feel inept – spoiling the joke. 'I mean, if we're his friends . . .' But then softly the men – Paul included – being to grin in the way that friends do, before they get to trick their friends.

It's colder and the sky seems to rest down against them: attentive, but wearying.

Paul understands the magician isn't coming. He also understands it doesn't matter any more. They won't leave: Simon, Barry, Gareth, Lucy – they'll stand here and he'll stand with them – they're all going nowhere. Together.

But that's fine, I'm just fine now. I know why I'm waiting for him: The Great Man – I'm absolutely sure of that. I know exactly what I'll ask him, what I need him to make me do.

ACKNOWLEDGEMENTS

Versions or sections of these stories have appeared in *Crime Spotting, The Book of Other People, Granta, Guardian, Harbour Lights, New Statesman, New Yorker, Ox Tails,* and the *Threepenny Review.*